Rising. . .*with bright new love*
Stars. . .*that work their*

'Take Beth

Tristan's sister went ... can't think straight around ... make her so nervous. Show her y... ...de, then she'll relax and your problems wi... ...be over.'

Somehow he doubted it. 'I don't have a good side.'

Nancy rolled her eyes. 'You've hidden it from everyone but you can't fool me. It's still there. You're young enough to have another family, you know.'

'Tired of loaning out your kids?' Tristan teased, using levity to cover the familiar pain of loss.

She touched his arm. 'You deserve some of your own. Don't wait until it's too late.'

One special month, four special authors. Some of the names you might recognise, like Jessica Matthews, whose book this month is also the beginning of a trilogy. Lucy Clark and Jenny Bryant offer their second books, while ***Poppy's Passion*** *introduces Helen Shelton.*

Rising Stars. . .*catch them while you can!*

Dear Reader

I'm delighted to introduce you to Bethany, Kirsten and Naomi in the *Sisters at Heart* trilogy. I've always enjoyed reading books with a common thread and wanted to create one of my own. Someday.

When a close friend moved to another community, I knew that 'someday' had arrived. While bemoaning the lost opportunities for spur-of-the-moment walks and the lack of a readily available sypathetic ear, I couldn't help but reminisce about my other close friends. I have a special place in my heart for those who accepted me into their circle when I, as a teenager, advanced from small country schools to one with nearly a thousand students. We laughed together and cried together, shared our dreams and aspirations, and weathered the storms on our way to adulthood.

Consequently, when I met Beth for the first time, I understood how important her friends were to her and saw how their early camaraderie shaped their lives, making them as emotionally close as sisters. They shared many experiences and interests, and from that this series came into being.

I invite you to meet three women whose friendship has withstood the test of time. I hope that you, too, have several friends who are your 'sisters at heart'.

Happy Reading!

Jessica Matthews

FOR A CHILD'S SAKE

BY

JESSICA MATTHEWS

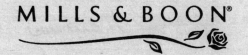

MILLS & BOON®

To Terry, with all my love.

First published in Great Britain 1997
Harlequin Mills & Boon Limited,
Eton House, 18-24 Paradise Road, Richmond, Surrey TW9 1SR

ISBN 0 263 80378 3

Set in Times 10 on 12 pt. by
Rowland Phototypesetting Limited
Bury St Edmunds, Suffolk

03-9709-44592-D

Printed and bound in Great Britain
by Mackays of Chatham PLC, Chatham

CHAPTER ONE

'THERE'S a kid bleeding all over the waiting room.'

In the process of whipping the soiled linens off the ER bed, Bethany Trahern paused at her co-worker's announcement. Her nurse's imagination conjured up all sorts of horrible images and she straightened to stare at the tall young woman standing in the doorway.

'Why aren't you—?' A picture of the young office clerk on duty flashed across her mental screen and she cut herself off. Now she understood why her efficient helper seemed so nonchalant about the situation. 'Let me guess. Rhonda.'

Katie Alexander, the emergency medical technician-trainee, grinned. Her brown eyes sparkled with merriment as she tossed her nutmeg-brown braid over one shoulder. 'Right as usual.'

Beth resumed her housekeeping chore. 'Figures,' she muttered, wadding the sheet into a ball.

Katie grinned. 'I never could understand why she accepted the job here in Emergency Services. Blood and the ER go hand in hand. As an admitting clerk, she should have known that people sometimes walk in with gruesome injuries.'

'I suppose she has her reasons,' Beth said, refusing to elaborate on her own motivations for choosing this particular job. Picking up a clean sheet, she shook out its crisp folds. Before the far corners of the lightweight cotton fabric fluttered onto the mattress she had expertly tucked in the bottom edges.

'How soon until we have a room available?' Katie asked.

'I'll have this one ready in a few minutes.'

'Should I move this one to the head of the line, or have her take a number like everyone else?'

'How far behind are we?'

'Far enough to know that we'll miss supper. Again.'

Beth sighed. If only Administration would agree to hire another ER physician. One simply wasn't enough. 'Check it out. Maybe Rhonda isn't crying wolf this time. If it looks more serious than the man with the broken toe and the woman with abdominal pain bring her in now.'

'You got it.'

Katie took off while Beth tidied the room at record speed. It was a typical Friday evening in Mercer Hospital's Emergency Room and although she liked to keep busy she preferred a less frantic pace. She hated to think of how many beds she'd changed since she came on duty at three o'clock—nearly five hours ago.

Beth had smoothed out the last wrinkles when Katie reappeared. This time, however, she pushed a small child in a wheelchair and had a statuesque brunette on her heels.

'This is Jackie Lane and her mother,' the EMT announced, parking the chair close to the small bed. 'Jackie fell out of her brother's tree-house.'

Beth took one glance at the bloody bandage taped to the youngster's forehead, the red splatter stains on her long-sleeved shirt and the scraped knee peeking out from the torn jogging suit leg. The admitting clerk had, at least this time, been somewhat accurate.

In the background a shrill ambulance siren came to an abrupt stop, signaling the arrival of yet another individual requiring medical assistance. With a slight nod and a raised eyebrow, Beth dismissed Katie to lend her services where they would be better utilized.

Pulling a fresh pair of latex gloves out of her cranberry scrub pants pocket, Beth tugged them on. Leaning over for a better look at her newest patient, she noted that the child was a smaller version of her mother. Pushing Jackie's light brown bangs to one side, she peeled back the home-made pressure pad as gently as possible. Considering the unseasonably chilly mid-September weather, she asked, 'Isn't it too cold to be outside?'

'I wore my coat,' Jackie stated. 'Besides, Keith said he'd let me climb the ladder when I turned seven. Today's my birthday. My foot slipped and I fell.'

Noticing how quickly the blood welled in the gash along the child's hairline, Beth pressed a thick square of clean gauze onto the wound. 'How far?' she asked, considering the possibility of other—and more serious—internal injuries.

'About five feet,' Mrs Lane reported in a quivery voice. Wrinkles of worry etched her thirty-ish face and her turquoise windsuit crackled as she wrung her hands and fidgeted. 'She fell on her left side and hit her head on the edge of the brick walkway. I was in the kitchen and saw the whole thing, but I was too far away to do anything to stop her.'

She addressed her daughter. 'You were supposed to wait for someone to help you.'

'Did Jackie lose consciousness?'

Mrs Lane shook her head. 'I don't think so. I was there within seconds. She seemed dazed at first, but never passed out.'

'That's good.'

The woman dabbed at her watery eyes with a tissue. 'I'm sorry.' Her voice grew stronger. 'I've had nurse's training and shouldn't be so emotional over this, but it's different when it's your own child.'

'That's understandable,' Beth consoled, wondering if she'd ever experience the dilemma Mrs Lane now faced. If her life followed the pattern of the past few years, she probably wouldn't.

She watched Jackie huddle in one corner of the wheelchair and noticed how the girl kept her left arm immobile. 'Does your wrist hurt?'

The youngster nodded, wiping at a tear trickling down her dirt-smudged face.

Beth patted her shoulder. 'Looks like you'll need a few stitches, my dear. We'll probably take a few X-rays, too. Just to see if anything's broken. Who's your doctor?'

'Dr Lockwood is my. . .her pediatrician,' Mrs Lane reported.

A feeling of dread spread through Beth's being at the sound of Tristan Lockwood's name. Yet, no matter what she thought or felt about him, her patients came first.

Keeping her voice even, she said, 'We have a very competent ER physician on duty but, as you may have noticed, we're swamped tonight. I'll ask him how soon he can see Jackie, but if you'd prefer Dr Lockwood I'll call him instead.' Her voice trailed away and she crossed her fingers behind her back.

Mrs Lane chewed on her lip and studied her forlorn-looking daughter. 'I guess it doesn't matter,' she finally admitted. 'The sooner she's taken care of the better.'

Beth struggled to hide her relief. With any luck at all, Dr Sullivan would be available soon. 'I'll be right back,' she promised.

She located a suture tray, then left the tiny cubicle in search of the gray-haired, soon-to-be-retired Amos Sullivan. It didn't take long to find him in Trauma Room One with Katie, two other ER nurses and a surgeon.

Skirting the ambulance crew and two uniformed police officers, she approached the gurney. The familiar odors of sweat, dirt and fresh blood grew stronger as she moved in for a closer look. The terse commands hanging in the air spoke of the seriousness of this particular case. From all indications, Dr Sullivan's attention would be required for some time.

Hoping that the situation wasn't as bad as it appeared, Beth asked, 'What do we have?'

'A stabbing. Upper abdomen,' the fifty-eight-year-old ER nursing supervisor—Rose Watson—answered as she adjusted the IV flow rate. 'A few more of his buddies are on the way in.' She glanced in Beth's direction. 'How are things out there?'

'Chaotic. I have a little girl who needs stitches and X-rays, and a number of others who are waiting to see a physician.'

'Better send for reinforcements, Beth,' Dr Sullivan announced, keeping his attention fixed on the young man lying on the gurney. 'I'll be tied up with this fellow for a while.'

'Sure thing.' Beth tried to keep the note of disappointment out of her voice. She might have known that Dr

Lockwood's presence was inevitable. With heavy footsteps and a return of an equally weighty sense of foreboding, she walked down the hall toward the ER nurses' desk. But before she could make the telephone call a leather-jacketed Dr Lockwood strode toward her.

'Is a patient of mine still here?' he asked in a deep, husky voice that matched his solid, muscular build. 'Jackie Lane.'

'Yes, sir,' Beth replied, her heart pounding at the sight of the man who had an uncanny ability to upset her calm.

'May I ask why she's been waiting for the past several hours for treatment?' The pulse in his temple throbbed, warning Beth of the pediatrician's unhappy state of mind. 'Need I remind you that this is an *emergency* room? The term does imply that some haste is in order.'

Warmth spread from her neck upwards at his censuring remark. A sarcastic reply hovered on her lips but she clenched her jaw. Arguing was futile, especially with someone in authority. That had been one lesson she'd learned early in her twenty-six-year-old life.

Beth swallowed hard. 'Your patient is in Room Two,' she said instead, returning his steady gaze with one of her own.

He shrugged off his coat, tossed it over a vacant chair and led the way. As in times past, she noticed how much taller and more robust he was in comparison to the short, portly Dr Sullivan. For a brief second she wondered why such a large and solemn man had chosen a specialty associated with tiny patients and laughter.

All things considered, the two physicians were a lesson in contrasts. Dr Sullivan wore baggy scrub suits to accommodate his paunch, while Dr Lockwood's stone-washed jeans and maroon polo shirt fit him like a glove. Dr Sullivan's balding head sported a few strands of gray, whereas Dr Lockwood's dark hair lacked even an occasional glimmer of silver. The shortly cropped style emphasized the younger man's high forehead and exposed a definite widow's peak. His eyes were deep brown like pecans, not green and somewhat faded.

The older physician had been blessed with bushy white eyebrows and a round nose. His appearance, along with an affinity for wintergreen-flavored breath mints, made him the perfect candidate to play Santa Claus every Christmas.

On the other hand, Dr Lockwood had eyebrows the color of sable, a straight nose and a squared jawline complete with the tiniest indentation in his chin. The scent of sandalwood lingered around him, an all-male smell which went unappreciated by his patients but not by their mothers or the female staff.

Dr Sullivan wore a perpetual smile. As far as Beth knew, Dr Lockwood reserved his for his small patients.

Outside the cubicle he paused. 'I suppose everyone else is busy,' he said gruffly, with one hand poised on the doorframe.

'Yes.' Beth raised her chin and gritted her teeth, refusing to reveal how hard his hint for another assistant had struck her heart. At least she had one consolation—the feeling was mutual.

He sighed. 'Then let's get on with it.'

Pushing the door open, he crossed the threshold and addressed the youngster. 'How's my favorite niece doing?'

'Not too good, Uncle Tristan,' Jackie replied, her lower lip trembling.

'What brings you here?' Mrs Lane asked, her features revealing delighted surprise. 'I thought we were waiting for the ER doctor.'

'Jerry was worried because you'd been gone for hours so he called and told me what happened. I thought I'd run by and check things out myself.'

'It wasn't necessary,' Mrs Lane protested, although her ready smile and relaxed stance declared otherwise.

'I know. I wanted to.' Dr Lockwood turned to Jackie and began his examination. 'So you decided to try out Keith's tree-house?'

While Jackie murmured her reply Beth's mind lingered on one word. *Uncle* Tristan. Her spirits plummeted. She'd never redeem herself in his eyes now. She rubbed along the right side of her jaw, tracing the upper outline of the port-wine stain extending down to her collar-bone.

As she had countless times before, she wondered what it was about this man that unnerved her so. Why did she become as inefficient and clumsy as a first-year student nurse in his presence? And why, after working at Mercer for over a year, did she still suffer from this apparently chronic condition?

It was his hands, she decided, watching him tip the child's head up to inspect the cut. She'd seen physicians' hands in all shapes and sizes, but none had had the same long, lean fingers, the same olive-toned skin and the same strong bone structure as his. His nails were neatly trimmed, reflecting the attention he paid to his hands—as a member of his profession should.

Be honest, her conscience interjected.

OK, she thought with some degree of irritation. It was because the man happened to fit her schoolgirl picture of the proverbial 'man of her dreams'—all the way down to his eyelashes.

She'd never forget the first time she'd met him. So shocked by the uncanny likeness, her wits—and her opportunity to make a good first impression with the handsome physician—had vanished. She had dropped a crucial injection of epinephrine intended for a young child in a severe allergic reaction, delaying the treatment for several tense moments. Thank goodness the child had suffered no repercussions, but her self-esteem as a recent nursing graduate hadn't been so lucky.

Her confidence had finally returned under the tutelage of Dr Sullivan, although it had the amazing ability to disappear whenever Dr Lockwood presented himself.

As for her romantic notions, they'd died a swift death. Tristan Lockwood may have borne an uncanny physical resemblance to her personal 'hero', but his temperament did not. Ever since the unfortunate episode she'd sensed his dislike and had tried to keep her distance. She knew better than to be where she wasn't wanted—another childhood lesson. Besides, a successful, well-known pediatrician didn't associate with a junior nurse who could barely make ends meet.

Beth brushed at her warm cheeks, willing the heat of embarrassment generated by the year-old memory to dissipate. Dr Lockwood's rich tenor voice brought her back to the present.

'I'm afraid you'll need some stitches, love,' he said in a tone as comforting as a warm blanket on a cold night.

'Will it hurt?' Jackie asked.

'Just a little. I'll give you a shot first and then you shouldn't feel a thing.'

He glanced at the stainless-steel stand next to the bed. Apparently content to see the sterile suture tray in readiness, he turned his attention back to Jackie. 'Shall we see if you've hurt anything else?'

With his attention diverted, Beth closed her eyes and stifled a relieved sigh. Thank goodness she'd laid out those supplies before he'd arrived.

Her relief faded with his next sentence. 'Where are the X-rays?'

She swallowed. 'They haven't. . .been taken yet.'

'Why not?' The muscle in his cheek twitched—an ominous sign.

'I didn't have an order.'

'Now you do. I want them *stat.*'

'Yes, sir.' Beth turned to the beige wall phone, punched a four-digit code and spoke into the receiver. Unfortunately, she didn't hear comforting news; he was bound to take it out on her.

She took a deep breath, turned and addressed his back. 'A tech will be here as soon as possible. They're running behind because of equipment problems.'

He looked down at Jackie. 'Is it OK if I fix your head while we're waiting?'

'Can't we just put a plaster on it?' Jackie asked, her eyes shimmering with tears.

Dr Lockwood crouched down to hug her. 'It will heal much faster and you won't have an ugly scar on your pretty face. You don't want the boys teasing you, do you?'

His comment made Beth even more self-conscious

about her birthmark. She fingered the top edge of the white turtleneck top she often wore underneath her cranberry-colored V-neck uniform tunic, remembering her own painful experiences with cruel children.

'Uncle Tristan knows best,' Mrs Lane coaxed.

'I suppose,' Jackie reluctantly agreed.

'*Will* she have a scar?' the woman asked in a low voice.

'A faint one. It shouldn't be noticeable since the gash is so close to her hairline. If you'd feel better with a plastic surgeon—'

Mrs Lane grinned. 'I trust you, Tristan.'

Dr Lockwood turned to Beth. 'Irrigate with normal saline, please. I don't think there's any foreign material imbedded, but let's be sure.'

Beth nodded. Pulling the requested bottle out of a cupboard, she cracked the seal as she scooted around his large frame in order to move behind Jackie. Resigned to his hovering presence, she took a deep breath, catching another pleasant whiff of sandalwood.

Conscious of his nearness and his silent perusal, she irrigated the torn flesh with trembling hands. For the first time in a long time she wished that she could turn away—hide the marks that had colored her skin from birth.

Intent on her technique, the shrill jingle of the wall phone startled Beth out of her concentration. Her hand jerked, and water sprayed out of the bottle in an arc, hitting Dr Lockwood below his belted waist.

Horrified, she stared at the widening dark spot on his faded blue jeans. 'Oh, my. . .' Intense heat flooded her face, making her feel as if she might spontaneously combust. At that moment she wished she would.

Beth stole a glance at him. Surprise and disbelief were

written across his aristocratic features as he, too, eyed the damage.

He drew a deep breath. Without a word he turned, took a few steps and snatched the offending telephone receiver off its cradle. 'Lockwood here,' he snapped.

Regaining her wits, Beth rinsed Jackie's gash with the remainder of the saline and wondered how in the world she had managed to accomplish this mishap. Her eyes burned with tears of frustration and embarrassment as she patted Jackie's skin dry with fresh gauze.

Spying a wet spot on the floor, she yanked a paper towel from the dispenser to soak up the small puddle. One accident per doctor was more than enough. By the time Dr Lockwood hung up the phone she had cleaned the mess.

Except for his pants.

'I'm so sorry,' she mumbled, addressing her comment to his chin and bracing herself for a scathing remark. She'd been in some uncomfortable situations around him, but never like this. And never in the presence of his *relatives*.

The dressing-down she expected didn't come. Without acknowledging her apology, he stated, 'You're wanted in the nursing supervisor's office as soon as you have a chance to get away. Feel free to go now.'

His curt dismissal sent a new wave of shame flooding through her. 'But what about—?'

Dr Lockwood brushed aside her question. 'I'll manage.'

For some strange reason his cool, even tone made her feel worse. She knew how to cope with a verbal barrage but not his icy calm.

Burning with humiliation, she nodded, washed her hands and left the room.

Tristan glanced at his older sister. 'Don't say a word, Nancy,' he warned, seeing her growing smile. 'Not one word.'

'I won't,' she promised. The grin on her face disappeared. 'But I feel so sorry for her.'

'*I'm* the one who has to walk around the hospital with wet pants,' he reminded her, donning a fresh pair of gloves. God, even his underwear felt wet. Maybe he could find a lab coat to wear out of the building. If a colleague saw him like this he'd never have a moment's peace as long as he lived.

Nancy laughed. 'It was an accident, Tris.'

He grimaced. 'Yeah, right.' Turning to the child, he softened his cynical tone. 'Well, Jackie, girl. Are you ready?'

Jackie's face reflected her fear and uncertainty, in spite of his reassurances. Nancy crouched beside her daughter and held her hand as the small girl gritted her teeth and clamped her eyelids shut.

With one of his size twelve Reeboks, Tristan pulled a stool closer, sat down and administered the necessary injection of lidocaine to anesthetize Jackie's skin. 'That's the worst part,' he told her as he tossed the used syringe into the handy biohazard sharps container.

Nancy hugged her daughter. 'Daddy will be so proud when he hears how well you behaved,' she crooned.

Jackie's shoulders straightened and a faint smile appeared.

Tristan began suturing the edges of skin together, careful to watch Jackie's expression. She frowned and wrinkled her nose but gave no other reaction. The anesthetic had apparently done its job.

'Is Beth new?'

Nancy's innocent tone didn't fool him. She was after information and wouldn't stop until she got it. 'No. Came last fall,' he said, enduring his sister's scrutiny.

'Hmm,' she mused, tapping her mouth. 'So why the sparks?'

'What?' He paused to stare at his sister.

'You heard me. Why does my brother, who's polite to a fault, turn into Oscar the Grouch around a certain nurse?'

He returned to his task. 'She's careless.'

'Haven't you ever been clumsy or done something bizarre in front of someone you were trying to impress?'

Tristan's medical school days came to mind, bringing along a few incidents he'd rather not remember. 'Maybe once or twice,' he conceded, before resuming his task.

'See what I mean?'

'It's not the same,' he insisted. 'The number of blunders she makes doesn't even compare. I know you're a nurse, too, but she doesn't deserve your sympathy. If you want to feel sorry for someone, feel sorry for the patients.'

'Now, Tris, you're being too hard on her,' Nancy chided. 'Beth was both efficient and confident when we got here. She didn't act flustered or scatterbrained at all. At least not until you came.' Her blue eyes narrowed. 'You've done something to her, haven't you?'

'Wait a minute.' He held up his gloved hands. 'She just gave *me* an unexpected shower.'

'Not now. Another time.' Nancy sounded exasperated.

'I'll bet you hurt her feelings. Doctors are always taking out their frustrations on the nurses. You aren't an exception.'

Tristan recognized her attempt to make him feel guilty and refused to rise to the bait. He tied a knot and clipped the thread. 'It goes with the territory. Nurses need to be thick-skinned. We don't have time to coddle them.'

'Politeness isn't coddling. She couldn't arrange for X-rays without a physician's order—even I haven't forgotten that.' Nancy straightened and crossed her arms. 'You need to apologize.'

'I'll think about it,' he hedged, hoping that his sister would drop the subject. Taping a fresh piece of gauze over his handiwork, he gave his usual instructions. 'Don't get this area dirty or wet. Come to my office next week and we'll take the stitches out, OK, pumpkin?'

'I'm not a pumpkin, Uncle Tristan. I'm a *girl*,' Jackie reminded him, wearing a big smile now that her ordeal was over.

He threw up his hands and pretended surprise. 'How could I forget?'

Jackie giggled. 'You're silly.'

He grinned and tweaked one of her curls.

A knock at the door heralded the arrival of a bouncy blonde X-ray technician. To his dismay, the moment the tech wheeled Jackie through the door Nancy resumed her apparently now-favorite topic.

'Beth is pretty. Wouldn't you agree?'

Four years of experience had taught him the direction Nancy's inquisitions usually took. It had been a long day and he wasn't in the mood to hear how he needed to rebuild his social life. He picked a stray rubber band off the counter and began stretching it. 'I don't want to discuss this.'

'Why not?'

'Do you hound Jerry, too?'

'Nope. You take all of my time and energy. Now, back to Beth,' she ordered.

'OK, OK.' Maybe if he indulged her she'd leave him alone. He closed his eyes for a second to think. Bethany *was* pretty. She had dainty features, high cheek-bones and a slightly turned-up nose. Her eyes were light brown with tiny flecks of gold and green, and her tawny hair tied at the nape reminded him of the lioness he'd taken Jackie and her brothers to see at the zoo this past summer.

She also had the same sleek appearance as the caged animal. Now that he'd made the comparison he realized that her eyes reflected a similar measure of wariness. Was Nancy right? Was *he* responsible for the distrust he'd seen? Or had someone else caused it?

In the next second he reminded himself to mind his own business. Nurse Bethany Trahern's life didn't concern him at all. He had his own problems—he didn't need or want to get involved with someone else's.

Nancy frowned at him as if a thought had just crossed her mind. 'You haven't said anything about her birthmark, have you?'

'Give me a little credit. I'm not totally insensitive. Besides, it's no big deal.'

She nodded, as if satisfied with his answer. 'She's the right height, too.'

Tristan stared at her. 'What do you mean by that?'

Nancy shrugged. 'She's about five feet seven or eight to your six feet. You two fit together nicely.'

'Oh, for Pete's sake,' he murmured, running one hand over his closely cropped head.

'You should consider asking her out.'

'What?' Quite by accident, he shot the rubber band across the room. It bounced harmlessly off a wall calendar.

She held up her hands to forestall his argument. 'You've admitted that her skin discoloration isn't offensive, she's pretty—'

'I didn't say that,' he protested.

'You didn't disagree.'

'No, but—'

'See?' She sounded triumphant. 'Take her to dinner and apologize. The poor girl probably can't think straight around you because you make her so nervous. Show her your good side, then she'll relax and your problems will all be over.'

Somehow he doubted it. 'I don't have a good side.'

Nancy rolled her eyes and tapped her foot on the linoleum floor. 'You've hidden it from everyone but you can't fool me. It's still there.' She softened her voice. 'You're young enough to have another family, you know. You're only thirty-two.'

'Tired of loaning out your kids?' Tristan teased, using levity to cover the familiar pain of loss.

She touched his arm. 'You deserve some of your own. Don't wait until it's too late.'

The door opened and the same X-ray tech wheeled Jackie inside. Thankful for the interruption, he grabbed the huge manila folder she offered and removed its contents. He'd rather cope with a medical problem than dwell on his personal life, or lack thereof.

'Let's see what we've got.' He scanned the hand-written report as he slid the forearm and wrist films onto the wall-mounted viewbox and flipped on the light.

'Doesn't look like anything's broken. You're a lucky girl,' he said. 'We'll wrap it and it'll be as good as new in a few days.'

As he finished the door opened again. Rose Watson stood in the frame. 'I'm glad I caught you, Doctor. We've just been notified of a car accident, involving a pregnant woman. Dr Vincent may have to perform a C-section and he wants to know if you'll be available.'

'Be right there.'

Rose disappeared. Tristan patted Jackie's shoulder. 'Save a piece of birthday cake for me.'

'We will,' the child promised as she hopped out of her hospital transportation and walked to the door. 'Come on, Mommy. I want to open my presents.'

Nancy followed Jackie into the hallway, looking on the girl's upturned face with a benevolent smile. 'I can see you're back to normal,' she mentioned, her voice fading into the background as they disappeared from view.

Meanwhile, Tristan strode toward the nurses' station, hoping that the mother and baby due to arrive weren't beyond human help. A multitude of possibilities, ranging from the minor to the life-threatening, crossed his mind. Regardless, he would do everything in his power—use every ounce of his skill—to restore this child to his or her family.

Beth sat on the edge of the chair in Elaine Miller's office and folded her hands in a white-knuckled grip.

'I hate to do this, but I have no choice,' the evening shift supervisor reported with an apologetic expression.

Beth braced herself for bad news. Rumors of hospital lay-offs had run rampant for the past few weeks. Being one of the last ones hired made it almost certain that she'd be one of the first ones to go. Unfortunately, she didn't know how she'd support Ellen and the baby or pay her school loans if she joined ranks with the unemployed.

'I have to transfer you out of the ER,' Mrs Miller reported. 'One of our nurses has had a family emergency—her mother had a stroke so she won't be back for several weeks.'

Beth let out a breath. She still had a job, thank God. 'Where will I be?' she asked.

Mrs Miller grinned. 'The place everybody wants.'

Beth leaned forward. 'The new surgical wing?' she asked, her pulse fluttering with excitement. She'd wanted that assignment since her very first day on duty.

The older woman shook her head. 'Even better.'

Beth frowned. What was better than surgery?

The supervisor sat back in her chair and crossed her arms. 'Pediatrics.'

CHAPTER TWO

Pediatrics? A hard lump formed in Beth's stomach and inched its way into her throat.

Merciful heavens, she'd see Dr Lockwood every day. No, make that several times a day. Oh, God, she wouldn't survive the mental strain.

'Pediatrics?' she croaked.

'I knew you'd be thrilled.' Mrs Miller wore a pleased look. 'Everyone usually is.'

Except me, Beth thought. 'Actually,' she began, 'I don't have very much experience with kids. Someone else would be better. . .'

The gray-headed woman cast her a benevolent smile. 'If I recall, you used the same excuse when I assigned you to ER. You've done very well.'

Not according to Dr Lockwood, Beth thought.

'Don't worry. You'll be fine.'

In spite of the woman's vote of confidence, Beth felt compelled to continue. 'I'm not sure. . .I mean, Dr Lockwood and I don't—'

Mrs Miller leaned forward, rested her elbows on the cluttered desk and clasped her hands together. 'You'll work things out. Whatever the problem is, it can't be too serious or I'd have received a complaint.'

'Yes, but—'

'Dr Lockwood is an excellent physician. He's gruff at times, but it's understandable. His pregnant wife was killed in a train derailment several years ago. Poor man never was the same afterwards,' Mrs Miller mused. 'Experiences like that tend to change a person.'

Beth understood the concept better than most people.

'So, if he seems hard to get along with, don't take it personally.' Unlacing her fingers, the supervisor picked up a pile of papers and tapped the bottom edge against the desk. 'I know you're busy this evening so I won't keep you any longer. Report to Peds on Monday. Mary Peabody will orient you to the department.'

Recognizing her dismissal, Beth nodded. Shocked by the turn of events, she meandered down the corridor toward the casualty department, paying little attention to the people she passed.

Why me? she wanted to scream. She needed to spend *less* time with Dr Lockwood, not more. Unfortunately, her choices were limited—getting another job with a comparable salary would be almost impossible.

'It won't be for long,' she murmured aloud. If she could survive living in the county girls' home during her teenage years then she could work under Tristan Lockwood's sharp eyes for a few months.

Nothing lasted for ever.

The instant Beth walked past the ER nurses' desk Rose cradled the phone receiver and brushed a graying lock of hair off her forehead.

'Thank goodness you're back. There's been a car accident involving a pregnant woman. Set Trauma One up with the fetal monitor. Ambulance ETA is two minutes.'

Beth's training superseded her personal concerns and

she ran through a mental checklist of possible medical problems. 'Head injuries?'

'Some, but I don't know how bad. I've already alerted an ob-gyn and a neurologist. Dr Lockwood is still here and, of course, Dr Sullivan.'

This time Tristan Lockwood's name brought a feeling of relief. No matter what her personal feelings for the man were, the baby would have a fighting chance with this particular pediatrician looking after him or her.

A few seconds later she found the room and the necessary supplies in readiness, owing to the efficiency of Katie and another nurse. In one corner Dr Lockwood conversed in low tones with Dr Sullivan. The younger physician's brows were drawn into a tight line, as if he anticipated a battle for this baby's life.

The siren grew louder, then died in mid-whine. By the time the vehicle screeched to a stop in front of the automatic doors several more physicians had joined their ranks—a neurologist, a surgeon, an obstetrician.

Beth and the others rushed to the back of the ambulance. Ignoring the brisk wind cutting through her clothing, she detected the burnt odor of rubber and the cloying scent of exhaust fumes, another testimony to the life-threatening condition of their patients.

The rear doors swung open. A fire department emergency medical technician jumped out, shouting, 'Let's go, let's go, let's go.'

Hands reached to pull the gurney forward. Its lower legs dropped, then locked into position. The EMT held the IV bag high and rattled off the vital signs. Beth grabbed the front corner of the trolley, intending to help steer it up the concrete walk and through the hospital doors.

She glanced at the patient and froze in her tracks. The familiar face, now bruised, bloodied and swollen, made her skin turn cold and her stomach twist.

'Ellie?' Beth cried. The note of fear in her voice was evident, not only to herself but to the others.

Dr Lockwood looked over his shoulder. 'You know her?'

Keeping her gaze trained on the broken woman, Beth nodded. 'Ellen McGraw. She works in Medical Records. She's also my. . .' her voice faltered '. . .room-mate.' Struggling for objectivity, she hurried to keep pace with the group as they moved Ellen into the warm confines of the building where, hopefully, they would save her life and that of her child.

'What happened?'

'A moving van's tire blew and the driver lost control,' the EMT reported. 'He crossed the center line and hit her head-on.'

'I want a CBC, type and cross-match for two units of blood, electrolytes and coag studies,' Dr Sullivan ordered in the background.

'Oxygen, eight liters per minute,' Dr Vincent, the obstetrician, added.

Out of the evening air, Beth spoke to Ellen again. 'Ellie, can you hear me?' She waited with bated breath, praying for a reply or some type of physical reaction.

'How far along is she?' someone asked.

'About thirty-four weeks. She's due around the first of November,' Beth replied, her voice quivering.

Ellen's eyelids fluttered. 'Beth,' she breathed.

Beth grabbed Ellen's slim hand lying on her distended abdomen and noticed her cold, clammy skin. 'Can you move your fingers?' she asked, taking a pulse rate at the same time.

Ellen obliged. The neurologist flashed a penlight in her eyes to check her pupil reaction. After a few more commands Beth had scored Ellen's response on the Glasgow coma scale. 'A ten,' she reported, encouraged by her findings. A score of less than seven indicated a coma, while anything over nine didn't qualify as such.

Beth grabbed a blood-pressure cuff. 'Pulse is 95, BP 110 over 60,' she reported, recognizing the increased heart rate and decreased blood pressure as ominous signs.

'My baby?' Ellen whispered, her eyes struggling to open.

Dr Vincent pressed a Doppler stethoscope to her uterus, his forehead wrinkled in concentration. He lifted the sheets covering the lower half of her body before he spoke. 'Ellie, you're bleeding. I think part of the placenta has separated, and the baby's heartbeat is faint. We need to perform a C-section now.'

The woman's lids closed. 'Beth,' she whispered through her swollen lips.

'I'm right here.'

The appearance of clear fluid—spinal fluid—trickling out of Ellen's ears sent a shaft of fear through Beth. She grabbed Ellie's limp hand. 'Pulse is fifty,' she reported.

'Take. . .care. . .of. . .son,' Ellie croaked, 'since. . . I. . .won't. . .' Her arms twitched involuntarily.

The neurologist lifted her eyelids again. Beth could tell that Ellen's pupils were becoming fixed and dilated—all signs of an acute subdural hematoma. It was vital that

Ellie's breathing passages remain open and that she receive a diuretic to reduce extraneous fluids. The orders came instantly.

'We need an airway. Protect her spine. Administer mannitol. I want a stat CT scan,' the surgeon interrupted.

Tears formed in Beth's eyes and she swallowed the burning lump in her throat. 'Just until you're better,' she promised, refusing to lose hope.

'Prom-ise?'

'I'll take good care of him,' Beth promised, allowing a few tears to slide down her cheeks.

'Positive Babinski,' Katie declared from the foot of the bed.

'We're losing her. She's down to a four,' the neurologist reported.

The drop in the coma scale and the abnormal Babinski reaction warned of a poor prognosis. 'Don't you dare give up, El,' Beth threatened.

The scene suddenly took on a surreal quality, almost as if Beth was viewing the situation through someone else's eyes. She heard raised voices, but paid little attention to the speakers' identities.

'She's seizuring.'

'Diazepam. Two and a half milligrams.'

'Call the air ambulance. She needs a neurosurgeon.'

'I'm losing the baby's heartbeat.'

'We need that CT scan and an ultrasound.'

'No time. Get her into surgery.'

'She's not going to make it.'

'Let's move.'

The gurney jerked forward and Beth clung to her friend. Keeping pace, she hoped for a miracle recovery, but her intuition screamed otherwise. Ellen's earthly time was running out like the sands of an hourglass.

The surgery entrance loomed ahead. Two male nurses swathed in sterile garb stood nearby like sentries, ready to take over. Suddenly Beth found it impossible to release Ellen's hand.

This was it. The final moment.

The cart slowed but didn't stop. Warmth surrounded Beth's cold fingers. She looked up and saw Tristan's dark eyes and solemn face. 'We'll do everything we can,' he said. 'For both of them.'

Beth pursed her mouth to still her quivering lips. Fighting for control, she nodded. Looking down at her friend who was closer than a sister, she stroked the limp, reddish-blonde hair splayed across the thin mattress and murmured, 'I love you, El.'

She let go. Tristan grabbed the metal frame and whisked Ellen through the double doors. In the space of a few seconds the team disappeared from view. Only the sound of rhythmic thumping as the wooden doors banged to a stop remained. The noise reminded Beth of a death knell.

She raised her hand in a farewell gesture. 'Bye, Ellie,' she whispered in the now-eerie silence.

A foreboding chill sent a shiver throughout her entire body. Rubbing her long-sleeved arms, she froze on the spot while trying to decide what to do next. Her shift wasn't quite over yet—it was only ten p.m.—but she couldn't leave Ellen.

Rose made the decision for her. The motherly ER supervisor approached, placed an arm around Beth's shoulders and led her to one of the waiting rooms for families of surgical patients. 'Don't come back to work tonight. I know you're worried about your friend. You should be here for her.'

'Thanks.'

'If we can do anything. . .' Rose's voice died.

Beth managed a small smile.

Rose squeezed her and left. Alone, Beth paced the carpeted floor, ignoring the comfortable chairs chosen to accommodate those with a long wait.

Anxious for news and too tense to read one of the well-thumbed magazines standing at drunken attention on the rack, she checked the coffee-pot in the corner. Although she rarely drank the stuff, she sipped it for the caffeine jolt. Her night was far from over and she'd need something to keep her going.

With her hands wrapped around the Styrofoam, she moved toward the window. Leaning against it, she stared into the blackness, past the bluish-white rings of illumination created by the streetlights, and into her memories.

She remembered Ellen McGraw's easy smile, her propensity for practical jokes and the way she loved being outdoors. She remembered how Ellen had befriended her when she'd first arrived at the girls' home, a scared thirteen-year-old still hurting from her aunt's rejection. She remembered how Ellen had gradually taken two other girls from school, Kirsten Holloway and Naomi Stewart, under her wing as well, enlarging their circle of close friendship to four. Four inseparable teenagers.

Beth smiled. They'd called themselves the Four Musketeers. Individually they'd struggled with school and friendships, but together they had been unbeatable. 'All for one, and one for all.' The motto had been more than just a cute phrase: they had lived by it, offering each other moral, emotional and physical support as well.

When classmates had teased Naomi because of her crooked teeth and her family's poverty, Beth had comforted her. When Beth had needed help with chemistry, Kirsten had tutored her. When Kirsten's younger sister had died, they had all consoled her. When one needed money, they all contributed.

Their pact hadn't ended with high-school graduation. While many friendships dissolved as people went their separate ways, theirs had remained strong through thick and thin. Their lives had been battered by many storms, but none had prevailed.

'Bethany?'

Tristan Lockwood's tired voice from the doorway derailed her thoughts and she straightened. Accompanied by Dr Watson, the fifty-ish neurologist who also happened to be Rose's husband, both men still wore their sweat-darkened green surgical attire. Neither had removed their caps; their masks hung limply around their necks, revealing whiskery shadows.

Their presence signified one of two scenarios. Ellen was either stable enough to leave under the watchful care of nurses or. . . Beth refused to consider the more final alternative.

She studied their faces. The physical details were different, but their expressions were identical—sorrowful eyes and drawn features. Without asking, she knew what it meant. She'd seen it often enough and had worn it herself on more occasions than she'd have liked.

No hope.

Yet she had to ask. 'How is Ellen?'

Under Bethany's gaze, Tristan rubbed the back of his cloth-covered head. How he hated this part of his profession. Yet he was relatively lucky. He had good news.

The moment Tristan had taken Ellen's infant in his arms, he'd known that he'd fight the Grim Reaper with every ounce of knowledge and every skill he possessed. He wouldn't allow fate to rob some other man of his child as easily as it had his own. While he'd been engrossed in his newest patient's fight for life, the medical team had struggled with the battle for Ellen's. Tristan soon had reason for optimism. The others hadn't.

The neurologist answered. 'I'm sorry, Beth. The brain damage was too extensive. I'm surprised she stayed conscious as long as she did.'

Beth chewed on her full lower lip and rubbed her arms. The glimmer in her eyes was unmistakable and she looked away to stare at the ceiling.

'We did everything we could,' Dr Watson added kindly.

She nodded. 'I know. Thank you.'

'If you need help with the arrangements. . .'

Drawing a shaky breath, she nodded again to acknowledge his offer. Deep in his gut, Tristan doubted whether she'd ask for assistance.

The resignation and sadness in her eyes nearly undid him. Dr Watson left the room and an undeniable urge to take her into his arms flooded over Tristan. But before he took a step forward Beth squared her shoulders and turned her doe-eyed gaze on him.

'The baby?'

'A boy,' Tristan replied.

The lines around Beth's mouth softened. 'She insisted

that it was. Wouldn't even consider otherwise.'

'Are you sure Ellen wasn't due for another six weeks?'

'That's what she told me.' She wrinkled her forehead. 'Why?'

He shrugged. 'We've assessed him at about a thirty-six-week gestational age—older than I'd expected.'

'Then he's OK?'

'I wouldn't say that,' Tristan hedged, hating to take away her audible relief. 'We're trying to stabilize his low blood sugar. We could probably care for him here, but since our Level II nursery hasn't been officially recognized yet I'm transferring him to a neonatal unit in Kansas City. Is there someone we should contact? A family member?' He cleared his throat. 'The father, perhaps?'

'No. There's no one.' Beth sighed. 'Ellen never told me anything about the baby's dad. Not even his name.' She'd tried on several occasions to get her friend to divulge the information, but Ellen had refused. Hoping that time would change her mind, Beth had let the subject drop. If only she had been more tenacious. . .

'You realize, then, that the baby automatically becomes a ward of the court. Social Services will make the decisions regarding his care.'

'I'm well aware of that fact, Dr Lockwood,' she said, her voice as stiff as her posture. 'I don't know if Ellen went through the legal motions, but if she didn't I *will* petition for his guardianship.'

Tristan blinked, startled by Bethany's vehemence and flashing eyes. This shy, quiet nurse who took everything he'd ever dished out without a word of protest had shown her claws. Once again he was struck by her similarity to the lioness—when something dear was threatened she would attack.

For a brief moment he wondered if on some subconscious level he'd purposely goaded her in the hopes of seeing some reaction—some spark of life. Now he had his answer. Underneath her cool and often clumsy exterior was a woman of fire, not the doormat he'd thought her to be.

He tried to reconcile these seemingly two different characteristics into one individual, but the side he was most familiar with raised his reservations where an infant was concerned.

'Caring for a baby is hard work, even for couples with support from their extended families. Can you handle it alone?'

'I'm a nurse, Doctor. You don't need to remind me what babies need.'

'I have to look out for the interests of my patients. The majority of them can't speak for themselves.'

She stared at him, unflinching. 'I haven't exactly been Ms Efficiency around you, but I am fully capable of taking care of this child.' Her face settled into a mask. 'Can I see him?'

He didn't hesitate. 'Sure.' He took her by the elbow and accompanied her to the nursery, saying, 'There'll be a lot of tubes and wires.' Although her training should have prepared her for the sight she'd see, he uttered his usual warning. Mechanical devices attached to bodies no bigger than one's hand were nightmarish to an objective observer; it often seemed cruel to someone with personal or familial ties.

Inside the anteroom—amid the smell of antiseptic,

baby powder and fresh linen—he went to one sink, while she stood in front of another. After a thorough hand-scrubbing, he slipped a clean cotton gown over his scrubs and handed one to Beth.

He watched her as she took it, unable to read much emotion on her heart-shaped face. Her hands, however, betrayed her.

She fumbled with the strings at the back of her neck and he brushed aside her trembling fingers to do the honors himself. Sliding his hand underneath her shoulder-length ponytail, he was conscious of its softness, and wondered how it would look if freed from the confining *faux* pearl clip. A faint floral scent drifted upwards and he noticed the graceful lines of her nape as he tied a bow. To his surprise, his body stirred and he turned away, catching the wide eyes of an interested nursery RN.

He frowned, sending a blush across the woman's face before she took a sudden interest in a stack of clean linen. So he'd never helped someone with their gown before. These were simply unusual circumstances—nothing to start a rumor over. At the same time, he was grateful for his baggy pants and the protective gown, hiding the physical evidence.

'Over there.' He pointed to a small glassed-in area closest to the nurses' desk. It was intended to isolate the more serious cases from the healthy ones—the area he'd worked night and day these past few years to establish.

Leading the way through the maze of bassinets and incubators set up with special bilirubin lights for jaundiced newborns, he breathed in the odors unique to this area of the hospital. The smell of antiseptic hovered in the air as in other parts of the facility, but here the fragrance of talcum powder and baby soap tempered the harshness.

Before long, Bethany gazed through the Plexiglas and looked upon the tiny form with IV lines, monitors and an umbilical catheter attached. His tiny chest rose and fell in an unsteady rhythm.

'Daniel,' she announced in a strong voice. 'His name is Daniel James.' Almost as an afterthought, as if she needed to explain herself, she added, 'His mother chose it.'

She hit the porthole latches with her elbows so as not to contaminate her hands. The covers swung open and she reached inside to caress the five-pound baby's tiny arms and legs. He jerked when she touched him. 'So precious,' she murmured. 'And so small.'

With her eyes shimmering and the lines around her mouth relaxed, Beth met Tristan's gaze. 'Thank you.'

Beth's throat burned from emotion. A mere 'thank you' seemed trite, but all she had to offer the pediatrician was her gratitude for this wonderful gift.

She couldn't take her eyes off the tiny human being. She studied his spindly arms and legs, the littlest fingers and toes, the peach fuzz covering a perfectly shaped head, the button nose and rosebud lips, hoping to find a familiar feature—some physical legacy from his mother. Her search was fruitless.

Listening to the beeps of the monitors, the occasional high-pitched sound of an alarm and the whoosh of oxygen flowing into the incubator, her heart ached over the loss of Ellen. If only her friend had had the chance to see her son. . .and the boy to see his mother.

Regrets, however, didn't change circumstances. She

forced her sorrow behind her and concentrated on the road ahead.

Familiar with the workings of the state's Social Services program, she knew the procedure to obtain custody of Daniel. First she'd file her petition. Since Ellen had been an orphan, Beth wasn't concerned about a family member wanting him. The only people who would be interested in Daniel were Naomi and Kirsten, but with both of them finishing their residencies they weren't in a position to deal with a baby. In spite of her precarious financial situation, she was still the logical—and the only—choice.

In two to three weeks, after interviews with social workers, the judge would make his decision and she could bring Ellen's son home.

Provided they don't think you're unfit, her little voice taunted.

Of course they wouldn't, she assured herself, stroking Daniel's downy skin and wishing that she could hold him. Yet she wondered if Dr Lockwood's opinion—as Daniel's physician—would enter somehow into the equation.

A shiver went down her spine. Considering their shared past working experiences, his description of her probably didn't include words like 'competent' or 'proficient'. Suddenly it seemed imperative to have him as an ally—to make him see that this child's place was with her and not with a complete stranger.

Conscious of Tristan's presence next to her, she drew a deep breath and began to speak, choosing her words carefully. . .

CHAPTER THREE

BETH'S quiet voice captured Tristan's attention.

'When I was seventeen my American government class planned a week-long trip to the capital. I looked forward to it for months.' Her smile became tentative.

Tristan leaned closer to hear over the background hum of life-support equipment.

'The fees had to be paid in advance so I scrimped and saved my money for what seemed like for ever. I worked at the public library after school and on the weekends. I even cleaned house for one of the teachers.

'The deadline for the deposit came closer and closer. I counted my money so many times it was ridiculous.' She chuckled. 'I guess I'd thought it would multiply under my mattress.'

Surprised by her humor, his own mouth twitched into a faint smile.

'But, no matter how I calculated it, I was going to be fifty dollars short.' With a gentle stroke, she touched Daniel's loose fist with an index finger. His tiny hand opened, then closed around it. Her benevolent smile grew larger.

'He's strong, isn't he?' she murmured, her tone more statement than question. Without waiting for Tristan's reply, she continued.

'I wanted to get another job, but our house mother wouldn't allow it. Said she didn't want me neglecting my school work. I was totally devastated; I'd wanted to go on this trip so badly I could hardly stand it.'

She paused. With a great deal of reluctance she closed the porthole to prevent the warm air and oxygen from escaping.

Certain that she'd reveal the point to her story in due time, Tristan waited with a sense of expectancy. Although he didn't consider himself gifted with an extreme amount of patience, waiting was something he was used to—a necessary evil.

He tried to remember if he'd ever had a comparable disappointment, but nothing came to mind. His parents, although not wealthy, had lived comfortably on his father's wages as a postal carrier. Obviously Ellen and Beth hadn't had the same luxury.

Beth's voice broke into his thoughts. 'Ellen had been saving her money too. She had a date for the junior-senior prom—the highlight of the year—and had picked out the most fabulous evening gown you could imagine.'

Tristan studied Daniel's tiny chest, noticing how the normal rise and fall was erratic and sometimes shallow. A second later all movement ceased. He straightened out of his relaxed stance, ready to begin CPR.

'He's not bre—' Beth said, her voice high-pitched.

An alarm went off. Before Tristan could enter Daniel's protective environment Daniel resumed his slightly erratic breathing pattern.

Tristan deactivated the offending noise by pressing the flashing red button. 'He's fine. As you know, sleep apnea is common in preemies because of their immature lungs. The respiratory monitor will alert us when he stops breathing.'

The concern on her face lessened, but the crow's feet around her eyes didn't completely disappear.

'You were saying,' he prompted, hoping to redirect her attention and her worries.

'Oh. Yes, well, to make a long story short, Ellen found a different dress—a cheaper one—and gave me the money.' Beth looked directly in his face. 'She gave up something she wanted in order for me to have a chance of a lifetime. Now it's my turn to do the same for her.

'Ellen hated being another statistic of a broken home and she was determined that Daniel wouldn't be one either. No child, Dr Lockwood,' Beth raised her chin, 'deserves to be cared for by people only interested in the money they receive. Daniel needs someone who loves him.'

'Paying for a trip isn't the same as raising a child.'

'No, but the principle is the same,' she insisted.

'Couples are begging for children to adopt. I know of several myself.'

Beth shook her head and poked an index finger into her own chest. 'Ellen entrusted her son to me, Doctor. To *me*—one of her best friends. Contrary to what you may believe, I take my responsibilities seriously. I won't renege on a deathbed promise.'

Tristan stared into her sparkling eyes, once again startled by the intense emotion she exhibited—emotion that, heaven help him, attracted him as effectively as bees to clover.

She laid a hand on his forearm, her touch whisper-soft against his bare skin. 'Do you understand why I have to do this for Ellen?'

He met her unflinching gaze, her brown eyes pleading.

Her faint, sweet scent drifted upwards and a tremor of excitement stirred his blood. For reasons he didn't understand his protective instincts emerged full force. After his long habit of shying away from all but superficial relationships with women, he'd thought himself immune to that particular feeling. Somehow this woman had disproved his theory, and he was stunned.

In the next instant memories of the months of gut-wrenching pain returned and he stiffened. No, he didn't want to endure it again—once in a lifetime was enough.

Beth's eyes continued to beg and his defense mechanisms kicked in. What in the world did she expect him to say? That he supported her decision? That she was doing the right thing? That it was better for Daniel to grow up in a single-parent household than one with two loving parents?

Tristan cleared his throat. Before he could speak a nurse interrupted. 'We have a problem, Dr Lockwood.'

A problem?

Beth dropped her hand and turned to face the nurse. Somehow she sensed this had something to do with Daniel.

'An approaching ice storm has grounded the LifeFlight from Kansas City. Children's Hospital wants to know if we can wait until the weather clears or if we want them to send an ambulance. If not, they suggest we try another medical center.'

Tristan pinched the bridge of his nose and frowned, his gaze lingering on the infant.

Beth waited, the steady whoosh of oxygen and the bleeps from various monitors continuing in monotonous rhythm. Finally she couldn't wait: concern for Ellen's son overrode her fear of offending the taciturn and often gruff pediatrician. At this moment she wasn't a subordinate, subject to the doctor-nurse rules of etiquette—she was a client.

'Well?' she demanded.

His grimace disappeared as he apparently came to a decision. 'We'll keep him for the time being. If his condition worsens we'll contact another neonatal unit. No point in putting Daniel or the medical team through unnecessary risk.'

With the decision voiced, Beth's energy flagged. Much as she wanted Daniel to receive the best of care, she was glad that, at least for the time being, he would remain nearby.

The nurse nodded. She hurried toward the desk and the telephone, the back of her cotton gown flapping behind her.

'You'd better go home and get some rest,' Tristan said, his eyes narrowing.

Beth straightened her shoulders, refusing to show any weakness. 'I'm fine.'

'We'll call if there's any change.'

'Are *you* staying?'

'For a while. Paperwork, you know.'

She licked her lips and raised her chin. 'Then I am too.'

His eyes widened in what she guessed was astonishment. She was shocked as well. She'd never been in a position where she didn't have to follow his orders.

He rubbed his whiskered jawline, the sound raspy and harsh. 'Suit yourself.' Without a backward glance, he strode toward the nurses' station, presumably to deal with the mounds of documentation required for the legalities of medical care.

Beth confiscated the wooden rocker in an opposite corner of the small cubicle and slid it across the floor until it stood within arm's length of Daniel's incubator. She settled in, promising to spend only a few minutes.

Although nervous energy kept her going now, she still had a major ordeal ahead of her and needed every ounce of stamina she could muster. Funeral arrangements had to be made, along with a phone call to Naomi and Kirsten. God, she dreaded giving them the bad news.

She leaned her head against the high back and stared at young Daniel. The room was quiet, except for the now-familiar noises emanating from the baby's incubator.

Lockwood never had answered her question, she realized. Revealing a small portion of her past hadn't accomplished a thing; she should never have gambled on his sense of compassion because he obviously didn't have any. Instead she consoled herself with the thought that she hadn't gone into more detail. She didn't need or want his pity.

I will take care of him, Ellen, she promised silently. One way or another she would. For Daniel's sake.

She closed her eyes and made plans. Luckily Ellen had accumulated a few clothes, a crib and a car seat, along with an assortment of other baby paraphernalia. With her friend's interest in her offspring's needs and her propensity for creating lists, Beth shouldn't have any trouble discovering what supplies Ellen had deemed necessary. Provided, of course, that the magical list could be found.

Minutes ticked by as she catalogued a host of things to do and people to see in the next twelve hours. Weariness struck, a bone-tired weariness caused by mental strain rather than physical exertion. She considered dozing in the chair, then decided against it. Even though she cringed at the idea of going home to an empty apartment, she couldn't camp out in the hospital nursery for ever.

Planting her white Nursemate shoes on the floor, she ignored her aching muscles and struggled upright. God, she felt dead on her feet.

Beth froze. *Dead.* The cliché now took on a sinister quality. Death wasn't something to joke about. Ever.

Pressing one palm against the incubator, she murmured her farewells to a sleeping Daniel.

'Going home?' Lily—the night nurse—who was close to Beth's age, bustled in and began her routine checks.

'Yeah.' Beth glanced at the wall clock. Two a.m. She'd stayed longer than she'd anticipated. 'I'll check in with you later.'

'We'll be here,' the woman replied, her voice perky for this time of night. She adjusted the earpieces of her stethoscope, before opening the incubator portholes.

Lily placed the chestpiece on Daniel's rib cage and Beth waited, unwilling to leave before the nurse completed the latest assessment of his condition.

'Good heartbeat. No temperature.' Lily consulted a clipboard. 'Everything's stable.'

'Thanks.' Beth stripped off her protective gown, wadded it into a loose ball and tossed it into the soiled-linen cart. The hallways were deserted and she quickly retrieved her purse and coat from the nurses' lounge. She walked through the emergency room and out the side entrance near the doctors' parking lot.

A blast of cold air hit her and she turned up the collar on her lightweight jacket. Yesterday's weather report hadn't predicted that a storm would arrive. If it had, she would have pulled a heavier coat out of the closet. Mother Nature seemed to be running amuck this year; long-lasting freezing temperatures didn't usually arrive so early in this part of the country.

Bracing herself for the six-block walk home, she added another concern to her mental 'to do' list. She needed a reliable vehicle. Ellen's old car, though excellent in its prime, stood idle most of the time. Beth's Toyota, moving up in years itself, had been the better of the two, but not any more.

'You're not walking, are you?' a male voice said out of the darkness.

Terror gripped her, her imagination fueled by memories of the assaulted women she'd seen in the emergency room. She spun around to face the unknown person. Sleeping in the uncomfortable rocking chair until daybreak suddenly seemed like a much better idea.

A tall form stepped out of the shadows, revealing his identity in the hazy glow of the streetlight. Her moment of heart-stopping fear disappeared. 'I'm afraid so, Dr Lockwood.'

He muttered something but the wind carried his comments away. 'At this time of night? In this weather?'

His gaze lingered on her jacket and her face warmed. At least he couldn't see her embarrassment. 'I wasn't anticipating a storm when I came to work.'

'Don't you have a car?'

She understood his surprise. In spite of its population

of forty thousand, Mercer, Missouri, had no public transit system except for the senior citizen minibus. Anyone old enough and capable enough to drive, did. No one walked, except for exercise.

'Yes. No. At least, I'm sure I don't,' Beth amended. Seeing his knitted brows, she elaborated. 'Ellen went into Blue Springs today. She had a meeting with someone about piecing her embroidered blocks into a quilt for Daniel. Her vehicle isn't in very good condition so I insisted she take mine.'

Tristan nodded in understanding.

A horrible thought crossed her mind. If her vehicle had contributed in some way to Ellen's accident. . . She swallowed. 'Anyway, I assume it's beyond repair. I'll check it out tomorrow. Today,' she corrected.

'I'll give you a ride.'

She started to refuse, then stopped. It would be foolish to turn down his offer. She might act flustered at times but she wasn't stupid. 'Thanks.'

He unlocked the passenger side of a nearby dark-colored BMW and held open the door.

Beth sank into the seat's soft confines, noticing the rich upholstery. Unable to stop herself, she ran her hand across the velvety fabric and inhaled the pleasant aromatic combination of a new car and sandalwood.

'Where to?'

She recited the address. Protected from the wind, she shivered and clamped her jaw to keep her teeth from chattering. For some inexplicable reason she didn't want to show her discomfort. The Tristan Lockwood she was familiar with would have some sort of scathing remark to make.

'Cold?'

Beth shrugged.

With the heater fan blowing full blast, Tristan pointed the vents in her direction. The warm air enveloped her like a down comforter, making her feel safe and snug. For the next few minutes she didn't want to think about the changes in her life.

The short trip passed in silence until he turned onto her street. Beth pointed to a small bungalow in the middle of the block and Tristan parked on the cracked concrete driveway. The building wasn't a candidate for a curb-side appeal award, but the rent fit their budget.

With one hand on the door lever, she was struck with a sense of loneliness. No matter how late the hour she'd always been welcomed by a lamp, left burning in the window. She hadn't realized how hard it would be to come home to an empty house, one that until a few hours ago had been filled with hopes and dreams of a wonderful future.

Tears gathered behind her eyelids. 'Thanks,' she muttered in a hoarse voice before she jumped out of the car, slammed the door and hurried up the walk.

With her back to the wind, she rifled through her purse for her keyring. Hampered by the pitch darkness, the familiar jingle acted as her guide. A tube of lip gloss and a small sewing kit clattered onto the cement porch before her fingers touched the cold metal.

The brisk breeze blowing through her clothing stopped, creating a sudden impression of warmth. She looked up just as a strong hand covered hers.

'Let me,' Tristan said.

Amazed by his offer, she stared at him and tried to find her voice. 'Why?'

He shrugged. 'The first time is the hardest.'

His perception was uncanny. Of course he knew how she felt. Only it had been much worse for him—he'd lost a beloved wife. She nodded before she realized that he couldn't see in the darkness. 'OK.'

His warm hands cupped hers and his fingertips brushed against her open palm before he lifted the object out of her hold. Seconds later she heard the scratch of a key inserted into the lock. An audible click followed.

Tristan pushed open the door, then reached inside for the switch. A shaft of light brightened the porch, illuminating just enough of their surroundings for her to locate her things and stuff them back into her shoulder-bag.

A minute and a few steps later she stood inside. As if sensing that she hated the shadows, Tristan walked through the house and turned the lights on wherever he went. Meanwhile, Beth hung her purse over the hallway closet doorknob.

'Everything looks OK,' he commented, joining her once again. Indecision flickered across his features. 'Will you be all right by yourself?'

She nodded, although she wondered what he would do if she said no.

'Get some rest.'

'I'll try.'

He tilted his head, as if unsure of what to do or say next. Reaching out, he took her hand in a firm grip and tugged with the barest amount of force.

She resisted, afraid that she had misunderstood his signal. Chewing on her bottom lip, she stole a glance at his broad shoulders. They beckoned, their size perfect for what he offered.

Her gaze rested on his solemn features. If she hadn't been scrutinizing his face she would have missed his nearly imperceptible nod.

Before she could talk herself out of it she walked into his embrace and buried her nose against his chest. Her eyes burned until she couldn't hold back the torrent any longer.

Long minutes passed. Beth took several deep breaths to regain her composure. She slowly, reluctantly, put space between them. 'Sorry about your shirt.'

Tristan held one palm to her damp face. Then, without a word, he disappeared into the night.

Closing the door behind him, she came to a startling realization. Tristan Lockwood might not show it but he had some compassion buried in his heart after all.

'What are you doing here?' Rose lifted her gaze from the chart in her hand to stare at Beth with widened eyes.

'Reporting for work,' the younger nurse replied.

'Are you sure you're up to it?' Rose asked. 'No one is expecting you to—'

'I'm fine. Really.' Rose's dubious expression prompted Beth to add, 'I took care of all the arrangements I could yesterday. I didn't see any point in staying at home to stare at the furniture, especially since it's my Sunday to work.' Her explanation held some truth but she had a more compelling reason—a lack of funds.

Ellen hadn't invested in a life insurance policy. The cost of even a no-frills funeral was staggering. Then there were the upcoming legal fees and Daniel's medical costs.

She couldn't claim him on her own health care plan until she had legal guardianship, and she didn't know if Social Services would pay for any costs incurred in the meantime.

Her precious Toyota had been reduced to scrap metal and Ellen's car needed more money to fix than it was worth. All things considered, debt loomed ahead and every dollar she earned was crucial. She literally couldn't afford to sit at home and feel sorry for herself.

Rose patted her shoulder. 'Of course. But if you find it's too difficult to be here, let me know.'

'I will.'

An assortment of medical conditions paraded through ER, keeping Beth busy for the next few hours. None of the cases were critical, but they forced her to concentrate on something other than her own problems.

While waiting for a teenage boy to return from Radiology with an X-ray of his ankle, a couple in their late thirties rushed toward the desk. The man, wearing a greasy mechanic's uniform, cradled a crying toddler in his arms.

'We're the Wellers,' he announced. 'Our boy needs help.'

'What's the problem?' Beth asked, studying the pale child for clues.

Mrs Weller held out a bottle of over-the-counter acetaminophen tablets. 'Sam ate these.'

Beth glanced at the label and sprang into action. She ushered the pair into the first available exam room and motioned Katie forward.

'Get Dr Sullivan,' she said, keeping her voice low. 'Accidental acetaminophen poisoning.'

Katie blinked, nodded then scampered down the hall. Beth followed the small family and asked, 'How many did he swallow?'

The distraught mother shook her head. Ringing her work-worn hands, she spoke non-stop. 'Can't say for sure. It was a full bottle, though—I'd just opened it. The phone rang, and when I came back the pills were all over the floor.

'I thought I'd put the cap on tight. It must have rolled off the counter and the lid popped off. Anyway, Samuel had a mouthful so I made him spit 'em out. But even after I gathered up every one I could find the bottle was still half-empty. There were a hundred to start with!' she wailed.

'Did he vomit?' The woman shook her head and Beth pressed on, 'Did you try syrup of ipecac?'

Mrs Weller shook her head. 'I don't have anything like that at home. This never happened with our other kids.'

'Ipecac is something you can purchase in any drug store. It's handy to have around,' Beth said. 'You never know when you might need it.' Now, however, wasn't the time to debate the merits of adding it to their home first-aid kit. 'How long ago did this happen?'

'About forty-five minutes ago. I was on the telephone. Then it took me a while to pick up the pills, call Hank and drive to town. We live twenty minutes away.'

Beth noted the time.

Mrs Weller's hand trembled as she patted Sam's back. 'Will he be OK?'

'The pain-reliever he ate is very toxic to the liver and kidneys. We've got to flush it out of his system before it does any lasting damage.'

'But he doesn't look sick,' Mr Weller interjected, his face pale underneath his tan.

'Even in cases of severe poisoning, there often aren't any early symptoms.'

Mrs Weller gasped. 'Will he—?'

'We'll do everything we can,' Beth reassured her. 'The sooner we remove the chemical from his body the better. Dr Sullivan should be here any minute.' Her mind raced through their options. Gastric lavage would be the best choice since too much time had elapsed for vomiting to be effective; some of the drug had probably been absorbed through the gut.

Anticipating the request, she didn't waste any time assembling the supplies. Although she hoped it wouldn't be necessary, she also prepared the suction apparatus in case the child's airway became clogged.

Dr Sullivan rushed in with Katie and Rose. Beth summed up the situation, motioning for Mr Weller to lay the tow-headed child on the table.

'Draw blood for stat liver enzymes, prothrombin time, BUN and glucose,' Sullivan announced. 'And alert the lab to get an acetaminophen level in a couple of hours. In the meantime, let's do a lavage then administer activated charcoal.'

Mr Weller pulled his wife out of the team's way. Samuel's hiccuping sobs grew to a full roar and Beth ignored his screams as best she could. The procedure wasn't pleasant, but the consequences of *not* doing it outweighed the temporary discomfort.

Rose held the child on his left side in a swimmer's position while Beth lubricated the child-sized gastric tube and passed it to the physician. The group worked like a well-oiled machine, with their movements orchestrated in perfect timing.

Dr Sullivan inserted the hose into the child's mouth, snaking it down the esophagus until it was positioned to his satisfaction. Using warmed normal saline to rinse, the cloudy stomach contents soon exited via the tube.

A lab tech arrived to draw the blood samples and left a few minutes later, her mission accomplished. Dr Sullivan repeated the washing procedure several times and Beth kept close attention on the fluid return. After what seemed an interminable wait, the right moment arrived. 'Looks clear,' she reported with satisfaction.

'Good.' He listened to the toddler's lower abdomen for a moment, then spoke, 'Bowel sounds are present so let's give the charcoal slurry with sorbitol.'

Beth twisted the seal on the small bottle in question, before handing it over. The elderly physician slowly dripped the solution down the tube leading into Sam's stomach. At the same time, he explained his actions to the Wellers. 'The charcoal will absorb and bind any of the acetaminophen in his intestine. Since there aren't any signs of a blockage we've used a preparation containing a laxative to clean out his colon.'

'Then he'll be all right?' Mrs Weller asked.

'He isn't completely out of danger, but I don't anticipate any major problems. The blood test in a few hours will tell us if we've gotten the drug out of his system before it was absorbed.'

'And if you didn't?' she persisted, her brows wrinkled into a straight line.

'We'll give an oral antidote called acetylcysteine every four hours for a total of seventeen doses. It might be tough getting Sam to cooperate but, unlike European countries, our Food and Drug Administration hasn't approved a protocol for intravenous treatment yet. We'll also admit your son to the pediatric wing so we can monitor his progress. Do you have a family physician?'

Mrs Weller shook her head and played with the frayed edge of her cuff. 'We just moved to town. I'd made an appointment for our kids to see Dr Lockwood next week.'

'We'll call him now. He won't mind meeting a new patient a few days sooner. Katie? See if you can find him.'

'Right away.' The EMT left to carry out his instructions.

At the sound of Tristan's name uneasiness swept over Beth. Thank goodness Dr Sullivan had handled this case. There was no telling what she might have done if the younger doctor had been here. Especially after what had happened last night, or rather early this morning.

She took a bracing breath. Until the episode in her home she'd only imagined what it would be like to rest in Tristan's embrace. Now she had a vivid memory of his solid arms holding her close to his rock-hard chest, his hand splayed across her backbone and his chin resting on the top of her head. Logic encouraged her to forget the experience but her feminine side told her that she wouldn't, especially after she started her new assignment.

'I think we can take this out now, big guy,' Sullivan murmured, withdrawing the gastric tube. An exhausted Samuel gratefully reached for his mother's arms, keeping a wary eye on the gray-haired man. A big tear hung on his lower eyelash, threatening to join the others already spilled down his chubby cheeks.

'Stay here until Dr Lockwood arrives,' the ER physician instructed the parents. 'After we receive the results of his next blood test we'll decide our course of action.'

Mrs Weller nodded and settled into a chair, with her son cuddled to her heart. Beth pulled a small blanket out of the cupboard and draped it over the child.

'Thank you,' the mother said.

'You're welcome.' Beth smiled down at Samuel and patted his back, suddenly picturing herself in the woman's place—cuddling Daniel. She couldn't wait.

Within the hour Tristan and a lab tech arrived. Although Beth would have preferred for Katie to assist the pediatrician, the child had been assigned to her care. While he conducted his three-year-old patient's assessment she took great pains to avoid his gaze—to concentrate on Samuel rather than on Tristan's comforting shoulders. She simply had to keep her wits about her.

Fate co-operated. For the first time in Tristan's presence, Beth functioned as efficiently as she did with the other doctors. A little slow, a little trembly perhaps, but there were no clumsy maneuvers. With a sigh of relief she returned to the nurses' station. To her chagrin, the two doctors followed. Each took a vacant seat on either side of her.

Rubbing elbows with Tristan caused butterflies to dance in her stomach, although she didn't know if habit or the realization of his tender side caused her condition. Perhaps it was a combination. Her hand shook as she recorded her nursing notes in Samuel's chart.

'You did everything I would have, Amos,' Tristan remarked, folding his arms over his crisp white hospital coat with 'Lockwood' embroidered in red script on the breast pocket.

'I'm glad he's all yours now,' Dr Sullivan remarked. 'Hey, what's this I hear about you stealing my best nurse for Pediatrics?'

Beth stiffened, her attention diverted to the conversation. She looked from one man to the other. Was someone else being transferred too?

'Who's that?' Tristan remarked, sounding mildly curious.

'Why, Beth here.'

Surprised by Dr Sullivan's high praise, Beth's face warmed and she rubbed the side of her neck.

Tristan seemed to take the news in his stride. 'I didn't know that,' he said. 'When?'

Beth's pencil snapped and she shoved the two pieces into a drawer. 'Some time next week.'

'We're going to miss her,' Amos stated.

'I'll bet.' His noncommittal tone didn't fool her at all. His face revealed as much enthusiasm as she felt herself—little to none.

The telephone jangled. Beth snatched the receiver, thankful for the interruption. A few seconds later she hung up. 'The Weller serum acetaminophen level is 175.'

Tristan rose. 'The cut-off for liver toxicity is considered to be 200,' he mused. 'Since he falls within the twenty-five percent margin of error we'll start the acetylcysteine, to be on the safe side.'

Before long Sam and his parents were on their way to the children's ward to face a stressful seventy-two hours. Beth wondered if Sam would still be there when she reported for duty. For his sake, she hoped for a speedy recovery.

With the next ER lull, Rose sent her to take a supper break. Beth opted to check on Daniel instead.

'He's doing great,' Lily reported. 'Hasn't had an apnea episode all day.'

'Good job, Daniel,' Beth praised him. 'Keep it up so I can take you home soon.' She addressed Lily. 'Can I leave a message for Daniel's social worker?'

The nurse tilted her head toward the door. 'Sure, but she just came in. You can talk to her yourself. If I remember correctly, her name is Miss White.'

Beth glanced in the direction indicated and noticed a middle-aged woman dressed in a navy business suit. She hated to stereotype anyone, but it was remarkable how this woman resembled the ones from Beth's personal experience—unmarried, with thin, angular faces and hawk-like noses. She wondered if this social worker had developed the same world-weary attitude from dealing with children enmeshed in problems beyond most people's comprehension.

She walked forward, her stomach a mass of nerves. Ms White had to look favorably upon her—a judge would base his decision on her recommendations. Before Beth could say anything the lady spoke.

'You must be Bethany Trahern. I was told I'd probably catch you here. I'm Edith White, Baby McGraw's case worker. I understand you're planning to petition for his custody?'

Although Beth had made no secret of her plans, Ms White's announcement caught her by surprise. It's her business to know, she reminded herself. 'That's correct,' she replied, feeling the older woman's beady-eyed scrutiny.

'I'm glad that someone is interested in this poor little tyke. But, even if you weren't, we wouldn't have any trouble placing him with a good family,' Ms White commented. 'Most prospective parents want newborns. You do realize, however, that we can't allow just anyone to take him.'

Beth's spirits dropped. Was this a warning?

'The court has to be sure he'll be in a good home—one responsive to all of the child's needs.' The social worker looked over her shoulder. 'Isn't that right, Dr Lockwood?'

Beth stared at Tristan, startled by his arrival. Had he and Ms White already decided Daniel's fate? Did she even have a chance?

Before he could comment the lady continued. 'Your nursing background will be in your favor. I can't imagine why a registered nurse couldn't handle an infant, especially one with special medical concerns. Can you, Doctor?'

Beth hardly breathed. If he said anything negative at all. . . With her jaw clenched, she fastened her gaze on his and waited for his reply.

CHAPTER FOUR

TRISTAN had never been afraid to give his opinions when asked for them. This time, however, he hardly knew what to say.

Edith White expected a glowing recommendation by virtue of a few initials—R and N. However, like all professions, letters after one's name didn't necessarily reflect the practical skill of the individual. Although Bethany had managed to function well on the Weller case, he still had reservations about her abilities.

He glanced at Bethany. She stood at attention, her backbone stiff and her fists buried in her uniform pockets. A worry line was carved in her forehead and fear shone out of her eyes. She obviously expected him to voice unflattering opinions of her competence.

Yet something deep inside wouldn't allow him to condemn her outright. It was tough to adopt children. Prospective parents were investigated for records of criminal acts and child abuse, had a multitude of personal references checked and endured countless interviews with social workers. Being a family friend, Beth might avoid some of the red tape but, even so, any unfavorable comments could diminish her chances of securing Ellen's son.

Knowing how much Bethany loved and wanted Daniel, and how other physicians and staff spoke of her in glowing terms, he couldn't voice his doubts yet. He'd bide his time until she'd worked on the children's unit under his supervision. Then he would know if his reservations were justified or if his sister's amateur psychology had hit on target.

Tristan stroked his chin. Focusing his attention on Bethany, he spoke. 'There are exceptions but, in general, I'd agree with you, Edith. A registered nurse should be capable of caring for an infant.'

Beth's shoulders slumped and her eyelids closed as if she'd offered a silent prayer of thanks. Which, he thought wryly, she probably had.

'How is the baby doing?' Ms White asked.

'Very well, considering his traumatic arrival,' Tristan remarked. 'To combat his hypoglycemia I've started him on IV glucose until oral feedings can maintain his blood level. He's had several apneic episodes—those periods where he doesn't breathe—so we're monitoring him closely and administering caffeine as a stimulant.'

He took a breath and continued. 'Oxygen and lung surfactant are being used to alleviate his respiratory distress.'

The social worker's puzzled expression made him explain. 'Lungs normally secrete a substance called surfactant, which reduces the surface tension inside. Without it the alveoli, or air sacs, stick together. When that happens they can't hold air and the lung collapses. So we provide the substance until the infant can produce it on his own.'

'And your prognosis?' Edith asked.

'I'm optimistic. The hypoglycemia should resolve itself in a few days as his body matures and he starts feeding better. Respiratory Distress Syndrome, or RDS, is a self-limiting disease and usually lasts from three to five days. By then the natural ability to produce surfactant usually takes over.

'He isn't home free, though,' Tristan warned. 'His apnea will require monitoring for at least three—possibly six—months. There are still the potential problems of infection and jaundice as well.'

'Does this breathing problem put Daniel at a higher risk of SIDS?'

'It's been shown that pre-term babies and those with prolonged apnea do have a higher risk of succumbing to Sudden Infant Death Syndrome,' Tristan began, choosing his words carefully as he gauged Beth's reaction. 'Keep in mind, however, that SIDS is defined as an unanticipated death without any underlying lethal cause. With proper medication and supervision, Daniel should be just fine.'

The lines around Beth's mouth softened, as if she found the news encouraging.

Ms White's eyes narrowed. 'You are capable of caring for him here, aren't you? If his condition should worsen—'

'Daniel will be transferred immediately,' Tristan interjected. 'We've been working on establishing a Level II nursery for some time. In fact, several of our nurses just returned from a specialized training course.' He grinned. 'The weather forced us to open for business sooner than we'd planned. Luckily Daniel's condition isn't as critical as it could be, or we'd have braved the storm to get him the care he needed.'

'I'm glad it wasn't necessary,' Beth replied, turning to study little Daniel in his safe haven.

Tristan nodded, his attention on Beth. Her benevolent expression mirrored that of his other tiny patients' birth mothers right down to the smile. A measure of jealousy pierced his heart. He'd never had the opportunity to see his son.

'How wonderful to expand your service to the community. I'm sure all the expectant parents are comforted, knowing that their sick babies can stay here,' Edith White said.

He pulled his thoughts together. 'We can't accommodate all of them,' he corrected. 'We won't deal with those needing specialties like cardiology or neurosurgery. Those kids will be transferred to one of the major medical centers, just as they are now.'

The social worker glanced at her watch. 'Oh, dear. Look at the time. You will keep me posted on his condition, won't you, Doctor?' She raised one eyebrow.

Her overbearing manner reminded him of someone who enjoyed wielding her authority. 'Of course.'

'How long do you expect him to be here?' the woman demanded.

Tristan glanced in Daniel's direction. 'He'll stay until he's gaining weight, feeding well and can maintain his body temperature. Anywhere from one to three weeks.'

Ms White tapped her forehead. 'Custody cases take about three weeks. To be on the safe side, I'd better make arrangements for foster care.'

Bethany's eyes widened. 'Foster care?'

The social worker nodded. 'I'm afraid so. We could license you as a temporary home, but it would take almost as long to process the paperwork. No exceptions, I'm afraid.'

'But what about his medical needs? His apnea? Can the couple you place him with handle that?'

The fear in Bethany's voice made Tristan reach out to her. He placed a hand on her shoulder.

'All of our parents have had first aid and CPR classes.'

'First aid? That's it?' Beth sounded horrified.

'Now, Ms Trahern, don't worry,' Ms White soothed. 'None of our parents have ever lost a child.'

Beth's face still held doubt and Tristan heard her mutter 'yet' under her breath.

Edith dug a business card out of her pocket and handed it to Beth. 'Have your lawyer give me a call. The sooner we get started the better.'

'I will,' Beth promised.

The woman disappeared, her lingering lilac fragrance out of place among the scents of disinfectant and baby soap.

Looking down on Daniel, Bethany's fingers brushed against the side of the incubator in a feather-light caress. 'I wish he could pass up the foster home and go directly to my house.'

Remembering her panic-stricken expression when the subject first came up, Tristan tried to lighten her mood. 'Sort of like Monopoly? Give him an "Advance to Go" card?'

The corners of her mouth turned up ever so slightly. 'Yeah. I guess so.'

'It's only for a week or two. Ellen would understand if you couldn't keep your promise for that length of time. Especially since it's out of your control.'

Beth raised her head and met his gaze. 'Have you dealt with foster parents, Dr Lockwood?'

He nodded. 'Several have brought babies and toddlers to my office for check-ups. They've been very loving and very concerned about the children in their care.'

'I'm glad you've had good experiences. I haven't.'

He hesitated. It seemed trite to tell her not to worry, but he found himself doing it anyway. 'Whoever gets Daniel will look after him.'

'I wish I could believe you. I want to, but. . .' Her voice faded.

He stifled the urge to pull her against his shoulder. 'Don't look for trouble,' he remarked. 'It depends on Daniel. If he's not well enough to be discharged then I won't release him. No matter how long it takes.'

Curiosity prompted his next question. It had nothing to do with a personal interest. Or so he told himself. 'Do you have an attorney?'

Beth shrugged. 'Sort of. I checked the *Yellow Pages Directory* and found several listings under family law. I have an appointment with a Peter Webster tomorrow.'

Tapping his forehead, he narrowed his eyes in thought. 'Never heard of him. What firm is he with?'

With obvious reluctance, Beth spoke. 'He's by himself. His office is on the east end of Fort Street.'

Tristan recognized the address. He frowned. 'Not the best part of town. In fact, someone got stabbed over there last night. And the day before—'

'I know, I know,' she said, her voice weary. 'There was a drive-by shooting. I'll be there during daylight hours so I shouldn't have any problems.'

Tristan bit back the objection hovering on the tip of his tongue. He had no right to dissuade her. If she chose someone from the seedier side of town to look after her best interests it was none of his business. Maybe this Webster would provide superb legal representation.

And maybe he won't, a little voice inside him whispered.

Don't get involved, his wounded spirit reminded him. Your only concern is Daniel's medical condition. You're not responsible for anything else.

Maybe not, he told himself. And yet, for reasons he didn't care to identify, he found himself suggesting, 'I know Mitch Adams has an excellent reputation. Why not give him a call?'

She hesitated. 'I. . .um. . .' Her voice died. Studying the black and white floor tiles, she rubbed the side of her face. Clearing her throat, she lifted her head. Without meeting his gaze, she nodded. 'Maybe I will.'

Tristan knew from her noncommittal tone that she wouldn't. In the space of a heartbeat he also knew why. Adams's firm, housed in a newly constructed building on premium downtown property, reeked with success. And success didn't come cheap.

'You really should,' he encouraged. 'Mitch is wonderful with matters like yours. People tend to believe his fees are exorbitant but they're not. In fact, they're very reasonable.' He'd make sure of it. Mitch owed him a favor—more than one, if he was counting.

'Oh?' Her eyes grew wide, confirming his theory.

He nodded. 'You'd like him. Of course, if you have your heart set on this Webster fellow. . .'

Beth shrugged. 'No.'

Tristan reached in his pocket for a pen. He scribbled his old friend's private phone number on a note pad.

Handing the page to her, he said, 'Mitch will take good care of you.'

Her smile widened. Then, as if a puzzling thought had occurred to her, a frown crossed her features. A question replaced the look of relief in her eyes. A question that echoed in his mind, even though it went unspoken amid the background sounds of Daniel's equipment.

Why? Why was he being so helpful? So considerate? And to her, Bethany Trahern, of all people?

Before he could frame a reply her face cleared. 'Thanks for the tip,' she murmured.

The tense moment slipped away. 'Any time.' With that, he turned away to hunt down Daniel's chart. Before immersing himself in nurses' notes and lab reports, he paused. Considering their rocky history of working together and the way he'd always kept his distance, his actions *had* been out of character. So why hadn't she voiced what was on her mind?

At the same time, he was glad she'd let the subject drop.

Because he didn't have an answer to give.

'Nighty-night,' Beth whispered to Daniel a short time later as he lay sprawled out in his cozy incubator. 'Sleep tight, little one. I'll see you tomorrow. Don't give the nurses any trouble. OK?'

Daniel blinked his unfocused blue eyes and brushed his tiny fist against his mouth. Two fingers found their way inside and his toothless gums clamped down on his new pacifier.

Bethany reached through the porthole and gently tugged his hand away from his mouth. 'Don't start any bad habits on me, Daniel,' she cooed.

She smiled down at the infant, memorizing his wizened features. These precious moments had to tide her over until she saw him again tomorrow. Although she'd rather spend Monday morning bathing and feeding him, she couldn't. At least not until she'd met with an attorney—preferably, Mitch Adams.

It was puzzling why Dr Lockwood had taken such an interest in her choice of legal representation. He'd never spoken more to her than was absolutely necessary, and never about anything personal. She'd wanted to ask him why he seemed so concerned—almost had, in fact—but fear had stopped her. Fear that he'd befriended her out of pity.

'You have the best baby doctor around, Daniel,' she whispered, watching him settle down for an early evening nap. 'If only I could figure him out.'

Daniel answered with a hiccup and a sigh.

The night nurse approached from the opposite side. 'Still here?' she asked, wheeling the cart holding the supplies and equipment used to monitor this particular infant closer to the incubator. After situating it to her apparent satisfaction, she readied the glucose meter for use.

'Only for a minute. I've got to get back. By the way, I've never thanked you for taking such good care of Daniel. There's always a nurse here with him. Is the nursery empty for a change?' Beth joked.

'Heavens no,' Ann remarked, cleansing the side of his heel with an alcohol wipe before poking it with a lancet. She shoved a test strip under the drop of blood welling out of his skin. Without opening his eyes, Daniel screwed up his face and wailed his protest.

'All done, sweetheart,' the nurse soothed, holding a cotton ball against the spot. 'Go back to sleep.' Daniel's fingers found their way to his mouth and he obeyed. This time Beth didn't have the heart to remove them.

Ann placed the strip into the glucose meter and pressed a few buttons. 'Getting back to your question, we'd planned to have one nurse for every two babies on this side.'

'Even so, I appreciate the VIP treatment you're giving Daniel. You enjoy working with these little ones, don't you?'

Ann grinned. 'You bet. As for Daniel, I'm glad you're satisfied with our care. Everyone's doing her best. Besides, we think the world of Dr Lockwood. No one wants him to fail.'

Beth wondered how he had instilled such a strong sense of loyalty in his nurses. He certainly hadn't endeared himself to her during the times they'd worked together. Yet a phrase puzzled her. 'You mentioned failing?'

The other woman nodded, placing a tiny spot plaster on Daniel's heel. She removed the used alcohol wipes, cotton balls and lancet, before closing the portholes. 'He had quite a battle with Administration over keeping Daniel.'

Beth blinked before she glanced around the room. 'But why? You have all the equipment you need, don't you?'

Ann nodded. 'Ready and waiting. Unfortunately, only about half of our nursery staff has been trained so we're covering the unit with a skeleton crew. As a result, the administrator and chief of Medical Services are afraid we might not be able to provide adequate service. If anything should happen. . .well, the legal people would swarm all over the hospital—especially Dr Lockwood. He's gambling a lot.'

Beth was speechless. The more she learned about him the more mysterious he seemed. She would never have considered him to be a risk-taker. Yet, at least in this instance, he was.

'It's been a dream of his to establish this nursery. He's been working on it for several years. The hospital finally agreed after we signed on another pediatrician—Dr Silverton—last spring. We're excited to get the project started.'

Ann's voice dropped to slightly above a whisper. 'I'm sorry about your friend, Ellen. I didn't know her, but she was one of our own. It's important to all of us, as our gift to her and to you, to take care of Daniel the best we can. It's rather poetic to have her son initiate this section, don't you think?'

Beth's throat tightened. She blinked away the wetness in her eyes. It took several long seconds before she could speak. 'I'm touched. And grateful,' she murmured.

The meter's shrill beep broke the solemnity of the moment. 'Fifty-five,' Ann remarked. 'That's good. We want his blood sugar to stay above forty.' She returned the cart to its designated place at the foot of his incubator before she spoke again.

'Is it true you've been transferred to Peds?'

Beth walked with her toward the exit. 'I'll start on Wednesday as we scheduled the funeral for Tuesday afternoon. To be honest, I'm nervous about the change. I really enjoyed working with Dr Sullivan.'

Ann apparently took her statement at face value and for that Beth was grateful. No one needed to know how Tristan Lockwood turned her professional demeanor upside down.

'Our pediatricians are wonderful, especially Dr Lockwood. He doesn't suffer fools gladly but he's patient with the kids.'

Beth struggled to hide her grimace, having first-hand knowledge of those particular character traits.

'Once you learn his routine you'll do fine,' Ann predicted in a positive tone.

Beth wasn't convinced. Yet she resolved to do her best—to prove herself to Dr Lockwood. She couldn't risk losing her job or chancing his objections to her adoption request. Daniel depended on her. For his sake she'd succeed.

Beth survived the next two days by keeping so busy that she didn't have time to think. Now, alone in Ellen's room with Ellen's things, her hard-won composure slipped. Dealing with the jewelry the undertaker had given her before the church service was more difficult than she'd imagined.

Through tear-filled eyes she studied Ellen's birthstone ring, before packing it away for safekeeping. The emerald was dull and dark, not the polished light hue she'd seen so often from its place on Ellen's finger. Hoping to restore it to the brilliance she remembered, she rubbed the stone against the neckline of her plain, black knit dress.

She checked it again. Disappointed over her unsuccessful efforts, she sighed. The radiance, like its owner, was gone.

'I thought I'd find you in here.'

Recognizing Naomi's familiar voice, Beth opened Ellen's jewelry box. She slipped the band into one of the slotted cushions next to the charm bracelet Ellen had always worn. 'Just tidying up a few things.'

Naomi sauntered into the room. Sinking onto the patchwork-quilt-covered bed, the springs made only a slight protest. 'Ms Neatnik,' she said fondly, 'you're making me lose my bet with Kirsten.'

Beth closed the lid and faced her dark-haired friend, recognizing Naomi's attempt to lighten her mood after the stress of the burial service. 'How so?'

Naomi smiled, flashing the silver braces on her teeth. 'We know your coping mechanism. Kirsten said you wouldn't clean house and I said you would. Here it is Tuesday, and I haven't caught you dusting since we arrived early Monday morning.' She shook her head and looked mournful. 'Now I'm stuck with cooking detail for two weeks.'

Beth grinned. Her friends knew her too well. 'No, you're not.'

Naomi clapped her hands. 'I knew it,' she crowed. 'I can't wait to tell her.'

'Tell what? And to whom?' Kirsten walked into the small room which was crowded with a double bed, an unassembled crib, a regular-sized clothes dresser, a chair and several boxes labelled 'Baby'.

'I vacuumed this morning,' Beth confessed.

'When?' Kirsten's eyes, one blue and one green, narrowed in suspicion.

'While you two went shopping for Daniel.'

'This is a set-up,' Kirsten protested, her auburn curls

bouncing as she plopped into the vacant chair. 'You both know how I hate to cook.'

'Cheer up,' Naomi advised. 'It's only for two weeks.'

'I guess,' Kirsten drawled. Then her face brightened. 'What do you think of the car seat we found for Daniel? What a great bargain. Lucky for us Ellen wrote down the names and addresses of some children's shops, especially the one specializing in used baby things. She learned the value of making lists from me, you know.'

Beth faked a groan. 'Here we go again. Another lecture on organization from an expert.'

'Speaking of lists,' Naomi remarked, 'does Daniel need anything in particular?'

Beth glanced at the three boxes stacked in the corner. 'I can't think of anything. Ellen had asked if I'd sew the baby a few things and she picked out fabric for several outfits. It shouldn't take long to whip them together.'

Kirsten surveyed the room. 'Cramped, isn't it?'

Beth shook her head. 'I may eventually move out the bed, but until then the crib will go in that corner.' She pointed. 'Ellen's dresser should be big enough to store Daniel's things.' She hated the thought of her friend's possessions relegated to a few boxes stored in the attic, but she had no choice. Lack of space in their two-bedroomed bungalow dictated that Ellen's things had to go.

'Why don't we do it now? That is, if you want to. . .' Kirsten's voice trailed off.

Beth traced the edges of the red stain along her jawline. Maybe it would be easier if they worked together. The small task might help them all adjust to their loss. 'Sure. Why not?'

Feeling somewhat like an intruder, Beth opened the top drawer of Ellen's battered dresser. Immediately she caught her breath.

'What's wrong?' Naomi asked, peering over Beth's shoulder.

'Um. Nothing.' Beth swallowed the lump in her throat as she handed a pile of soft cotton undergarments to Naomi. 'I'd forgotten how Ellen always kept a bar of scented soap with her clothes. The wildflower fragrance caught me off guard. It almost seemed like she was here.' Blinking several times to keep her eyes dry, Beth passed another handful to Naomi.

As if sensing that she needed a diversion, Naomi provided one. 'Kirsty and I checked on this Tristan Lockwood. He's supposedly an excellent pediatrician.'

'He is,' Beth agreed, keeping her tone noncommittal as she avoided her friends' gazes.

Kirsten and Naomi looked at each other. 'There's a "but", isn't there?' Kirsten coaxed.

Beth paused. 'He makes me nervous and I do crazy things. Just the other day I gave him a saline bath. Unfortunately I've been transferred to Peds. I start tomorrow.'

'You're trying too hard. Just relax. He's not any different from any other physician,' Naomi advised.

But he is, Beth thought. In spite of the tension between them—a tension that kept her infatuation in check—she was extremely aware of his masculinity. Memories of his embrace surfaced with surprising regularity, especially in her weak moments.

Apparently considering the subject of Beth's problems with Tristan Lockwood now closed, Kirsten changed the subject. 'I'm glad you'll be petitioning for Daniel's custody,' she remarked, holding sleepers and tiny undershirts out for Beth to stack in the vacated space. 'Though I wish we were in a better position to help you.'

'I'll manage.'

'You'll need a break every so often. Most new moms do,' Naomi said in her matter-of-fact doctor voice. 'We'll come whenever we have a weekend off. Besides, I'm looking forward to being an aunt.'

Beth smiled. 'I never thought I'd actually be responsible for a baby. I'd always planned on a husband first. One that wouldn't mind about this.' She brushed at her flawed neck.

'So things happened backwards,' Kirsten remarked. 'Life doesn't always turn out the way we plan. And, anyway, a man who can't look further than skin-deep isn't good enough for you.' She opened another box.

'I know. It doesn't make sense, but somehow I feel guilty about keeping Daniel. I'm going to enjoy him when his own mother can't,' Beth commented.

Naomi, ever practical, interrupted. 'You were Ellen's choice—don't ever forget it.'

Beth nodded.

Kirsten began folding a flannel receiving blanket. 'I wonder why El never told us about Daniel's father. I'd have thought she'd have at least mentioned *something* about him.'

'She never did,' Beth admitted. 'I asked, but she'd get a funny look on her face and change the subject.'

'Do you think it was a one-night stand?' Naomi asked, her brow furrowed. 'A heat-of-the-moment kind of relationship?'

Beth shook her head. 'No. Ellen wanted the family

life she never had.' Just like me, she added silently. She closed the fourth drawer. 'We can speculate all day but we won't get anywhere. Ellen didn't talk about him so we don't have a clue to his identity. He could be anyone.'

'Does your lawyer think Daniel's mystery dad could pose a problem with the legal proceedings?'

Beth recalled her meeting with Mitch Adams. 'No.' The young attorney hadn't been overly concerned but as he'd explained, 'Each judge is different; some are more cautious than others when dealing with adoptions. Let's not worry unnecessarily.'

She opened the bottom drawer and buried her hands underneath a neatly folded stack of shirts and sweaters. Her fingers bumped into something hard. Intrigued, she burrowed through the garments.

A small antique cigar box with an elaborate carving on the lid came into view. 'Oh, my goodness,' Beth exclaimed, holding it up for the others' benefit. 'This is Ellen's keepsake chest. I haven't seen it since we were kids in the Home. She stored her most prized possessions in here.'

'Quick. Let's see what's inside,' Naomi and Kirsten echoed each other.

Beth sat on the edge of the bed. With the container on her lap, she tried to slide the metal latch to the left. 'It's locked.'

'Where's the key?' Kirsten asked.

'Look in her jewelry case,' Naomi suggested.

Kirsten rifled through Ellen's necklaces and bracelets. 'Nothing in here.'

'Let's see.' Naomi tapped her forehead. 'Where would Ellen hide a key?'

Kirsten's face brightened. 'How about the desk?'

With her attention riveted on the chest, Beth shrugged. 'Be my guest.'

Kirsten darted out of the room, returning in a few minutes. Her expression was as disappointed as her tone of voice. 'No luck.' Her face lit up once again. 'I've never picked a lock before, but between the three of us. . .'

'No.' Beth's raised voice surprised herself as much as her two friends. 'No,' she repeated in a softer manner, knowing she needed to explain her objections. 'It's an heirloom. This box belonged to her grandmother and now it passes to Daniel. I won't break it to satisfy anyone's curiosity. The key will turn up. When it does we'll open it.'

'Beth's right,' Naomi remarked. 'Whatever is inside can wait.'

Beth traced the grooves with her fingers before she returned the antique to the bottom drawer. Deep down she felt relief at the reprieve. Privacy had been in short supply during their days in the Home; the girls had sought it in the most innovative ways. Going through someone else's possessions, however meager, ranked high on the roster of unforgivable offenses.

Today, although she had no choice, she'd invaded Ellen's privacy. Somehow it didn't seem right to examine Ellen's most treasured memorabilia so soon after her death.

For a fleeting moment she hoped that the key would remain hidden for a long time.

CHAPTER FIVE

'How's the throat, Millie?' Beth asked on her change-of-shift rounds the next afternoon.

'Hurts,' the five-year-old replied.

Beth wasn't surprised. It would be some time before the pain from her tonsillectomy went away. 'How about some ice to suck on?'

Millie made a face.

'A Popsicle,' Beth suggested, taking in Mrs Dodd's weary appearance.

The girl's eyes lit up. 'Cherry.'

'What's your second choice? In case they're all gone.'

'Orange,' Millie whispered.

'Good enough. I'll be back in a jiffy.' Beth strode to the ward's kitchenette and peeked into the freezer compartment of the refrigerator. Millie was in luck; two unopened cartons of cherry and orange Popsicles were nestled between several ice-cube trays.

A few minutes later Beth presented the frozen treat with a flourish. While Millie sucked on the flavored ice Beth addressed her mother. 'How are you doing?'

The forty-ish Mrs Dodd gave a wan smile. 'I'm fine. A little tired, maybe.' She sighed. 'The doctor told us she'd be in the ambulatory surgery center, stay a few hours for recovery and then go home. No big deal.'

'That's usually the case.'

Mrs Dodd glanced at her fair-haired daughter,

engrossed both in her Popsicle and a television cartoon. 'Please don't think I'm complaining. If she was bleeding more than the doctors expected I'm glad they decided to admit her. It's just that I wasn't emotionally prepared for any complications.'

Beth sympathized. 'She's doing well now. The main thing is to keep her quiet and be alert for any changes.'

'When will Dr Lockwood be in?'

'Around six.' According to Mary Peabody, the senior pediatrics nurse, he was punctual to a fault. After learning his schedule, Beth had considered taking her evening meal break while he made his rounds. In the next instant she decided against it. She'd never prove herself if she avoided him. 'If I hear otherwise I'll let you know,' Beth said.

On the way to her next patient she considered her first day, or rather her first evening, on the children's unit. None of her charges was critically ill and most had their parents to keep them occupied. The ward was quiet, making ideal conditions for a new person to become acquainted with the routine.

Although she'd been warned to enjoy the slower pace while it lasted, at this moment she wished for more activity. Maybe then she could forget Daniel's latest problem—forget seeing him lying in his incubator with his eyes covered as he soaked up healing rays from the bilirubin light.

Beth knew all about physiological jaundice. It was a common phenomenon among newborns because of their immature liver function, and they recovered without any lasting effects. Although the chances were slim that Daniel would develop a high enough blood level of the yellow bile pigment to damage any brain cells she still waited for each bilirubin result with bated breath.

She glanced at her watch. In about two hours she'd be due for her supper break and she could check on him again.

Turning the corner into Room 416, she heard her patient's father reading a story. She waited to speak until Mr Reed stopped to turn the page. 'Hi, Phillip. It's Beth. How are you doing?'

The three-year-old boy turned his head in her direction, the white bandages covering his eyes a vivid contrast to the dark skin of his African-American heritage. 'Daddy's readin' me a story 'bout free pigs. It's got a wolf, too.'

Beth acted suitably excited. 'Sounds like a neat book. How do your eyes feel?'

'Itchy,' came the boy's reply. 'But I don' touch 'em. Daddy an' the doctor said not to so's they can heal up. Don' wanna wear them old glasses any more.'

'I'm proud of you,' Beth encouraged him. Phillip's eyes had turned outward, requiring measures like patches and corrective lenses. Unfortunately the non-invasive methods hadn't worked and surgery had become a necessity rather than an option.

'Is it 'bout time ta eat?' Phillip asked, his hopefulness evident.

'You just had a snack,' his father chided.

'I'm still hungry.'

Beth laughed. Touching the boy's shoulder, she said, 'Soon. Very soon.'

Mary cornered her the minute she stepped into the hallway. 'ER is sending us one of Dr Lockwood's four-year-old patients—a Toby Hill. It's standing room only downstairs so they're trying to divert as many patients as possible. Doctor will meet them in our exam room. One of our aides is on her way to help you.'

By the time Beth had done a hasty check of the examination room and had returned to the nurses' station the passenger elevator doors whooshed open. Katie Alexander herded the family forward—a petite woman with a sandy-haired boy in her arms and a tall slender man.

'Beth will take over now,' Katie told the Hills. 'Dr Lockwood will be here shortly.' With that, she left.

Beth led them to the cubicle. 'What seems to be the problem?' she asked, motioning for Mrs Hill to sit on the exam table with Toby in her lap.

'He has trouble swallowing and complains of a sore throat,' Mrs Hill reported, slipping the youngster's arms out of his coat. 'He's had strep throat and tonsillitis before, but he's never looked like this.'

'This' included an extended neck—reminding her of the way a turtle poked his head out of his shell—excessive drooling and very slow breathing. The child definitely presented with some odd signs.

Heat emanated from his small body. She inserted the ear thermometer, anticipating a high result. A few seconds and a beep later the numbers appearing on the digital display confirmed her suspicion—104° Fahrenheit.

Although she expected Tristan and mentally braced herself for his arrival, his appearance in the doorway startled her. Don't screw up, she admonished herself.

Mrs Hill repeated her observations for his benefit while he scanned the details Beth had recorded.

Warning flags waved in Beth's mind. This child was seriously ill. The symptoms she'd observed were important, but the condition they represented eluded her.

Tristan bent over Toby to examine him. 'Does he lie down or prefer to sit up?'

'I've been holding him. He gets very upset, otherwise,' his mother reported.

'Can you open your mouth?' he asked the toddler.

Toby shook his head and snuggled closer to his mother. 'Go on,' she encouraged him.

'It's not necessary,' Tristan said. Before Beth could puzzle out his unorthodox examination he spoke again. This time his voice held urgency.

'I suspect your son has a bacterial infection, involving the mucous membranes of the epiglottis. This is the small, leaf-shaped piece of cartilage situated behind the root of the tongue. Its function is to close off the air passage when swallowing so that food won't enter the lungs.

'In Toby's case,' he continued, 'the danger is that the swollen membranes can completely obstruct his air supply.'

The life-threatening diagnosis spurred Beth into action. Maintaining an airway was paramount. As unobtrusively as possible she located an emergency tracheotomy kit and an intubation tray for inserting a breathing tube. She placed them on the counter within arm's reach, while glancing around the room to locate the drug cabinet.

She'd wondered why Tristan hadn't insisted on looking in Toby's throat—now she knew. Any manipulation could cause the larynx to spasm and close, cutting off his air.

Mr Hill laid one large beefy hand on his wife's petite

shoulders. She stifled a sob. Her fingers shook as she stroked her son's light brown hair.

'His condition is treatable with antibiotics but, as a precaution, we need to insert a tube through his nose and into the trachea. I'd prefer to do it now rather than wait until it becomes an emergency situation. It's much safer for him, too.'

Mr Hill's voice was hoarse. 'Do whatever you think is best.'

'Everything will be done in the operating room. It's very important that he doesn't fight us so we'll give him general anesthesia. While he's under we'll do a bronchoscopy first to look at the air passages. Then we'll insert the breathing tube, start the IV, get the lab tests and whatever else is necessary. He won't feel a thing.'

The Hills nodded. 'We understand. How long will he have this tube in?'

'At least three days. We don't want to remove it too soon and risk having to reinsert it. The worst of the inflammation will disappear in twenty-four hours, but his throat will need some time to return to normal.'

The Hills fell silent.

'Why don't you carry him downstairs?' Tristan asked as if he didn't expect them to refuse. 'You can stay with him until we sedate him.'

Tristan turned to Beth. 'Notify OR. Call Radiology—I want a portable lateral neck film stat. Get the lab down there for a CBC and blood cultures. I also want amoxicillin and chloramphenicol started as soon as we establish an IV. Got that?'

'Yes,' Beth answered, noticing Mary's entrance out of the corner of one eye.

'I don't want him left alone for a *second,*' he emphasized.

The senior nurse interrupted. 'Why don't you go with them, Beth? I'll alert everyone while you're on your way.' Beth stole a glance at Tristan.

With an impatient shrug, he turned toward the door. 'Let's go.'

At the last second Beth grabbed the tracheotomy tray and followed the family to the service elevators. The trip to the operating suite only took a few minutes, but she didn't want to be caught unprepared.

She was standing next to Tristan as the elevator doors closed. Beth clutched the sterile pack to her chest. Her attention alternated between Toby, the floor numbers appearing in the lighted display and the man beside her. The scent of sandalwood drifted toward her, its potency reminding her of the night he'd driven her home.

In the twinkling of an eye the elevator jerked to a stop. Beth's knees buckled and she lost her balance. Before she could regain it Tristan grabbed her. For a few frozen seconds his strong arms surrounded her. 'Are you OK?'

She nodded, every nerve ending aware of his proximity. Feeling strange, she moved and his hands fell away.

Tristan addressed the Hills. 'How about you?'

'We're fine,' Mr Hill reported, 'but what happened?'

Beth glanced at the floor display. The number two—their destination—glowed red, but the doors didn't open.

'I'm not sure,' Tristan answered, punching buttons on the control panel and obtaining no response. He repeated the process, to no avail.

'I can't believe this,' he muttered. He glanced at Beth,

then at her small bundle. 'I hope we won't have to use that.'

'Me, too.'

Mrs Hill's eyes grew wild. She began to pace, bouncing Toby up and down in her agitation. 'What are we going to do? My baby's going to die while we're stuck here. I can't stand this.'

Beth turned to the woman. Taking her by the shoulders, she spoke sternly. 'Nothing will happen. Toby will be fine as long as you stay calm. Take a few deep breaths and just relax.' She paused. 'He can sense if you're scared so pull yourself together.'

Mrs Hill swallowed, then nodded. The wild look disappeared from her eyes.

With the near-disaster averted, Beth faced Tristan. He pressed the emergency button and a clanging noise filled the air. Toby raised his head from his mother's shoulder. His fever-glazed eyes grew wide and his lower lip quivered.

'He hates sirens,' Mr Hill reported. 'Scare him to death.'

Tristan released the pressure and the noise ceased. Toby relaxed. Beth glanced at Tristan, certain that his thoughts matched hers. They were trapped and unable to summon help.

'Let's hope someone heard the alarm and reported the problem,' Tristan whispered, his voice grim. 'I can't risk upsetting Toby. With all due respect to our housekeeping staff, an elevator isn't the ideal surgery suite.'

Beth nodded her agreement. 'We're on—or at least close to—the second floor,' she pointed out. 'Maybe we only need to pry the doors open.' She searched the pockets of her pediatric smock—a white and blue teddy-bear-print apron which covered her cranberry scrub shirt. The only tools she found were a stainless-steel hemostat and a pair of bandage scissors.

'It's better than nothing,' he said, taking the hemostat out of her hand.

Mr Hill moved to the front. 'What can I do?'

'Help your wife keep him calm,' Tristan replied. 'And let us know if he acts as if he can't breathe.'

He wedged the metal instrument into the crack between the doors until the tiniest space became visible. Beth dug her fingertips into the small opening and pushed with all her might while Tristan did the same.

The space grew wider by fractions of an inch. By the time the hemostat clattered to their feet the slit had become large enough to accommodate their fingers. With a few more tugs the metal barriers gave way.

For reasons Beth didn't understand—and refused to question—the doors to the elevator shaft stood open. To her dismay, a three-foot drop separated them from safety on the second floor.

She stepped back. Leaning against the wall, she closed her eyes and tried to fight the vertigo overtaking her. It's only thirty-six inches—one yard—a little under one meter, she told herself, breathing deeply. No big deal. Think of your patient, not your fears.

Tristan faced the small group. 'I'm going to jump down, then you can pass Toby to me. I'll get him into OR and send someone after you. OK?'

The adults nodded. Beth thought the idea an excellent one.

Tristan patted Toby's back. 'You'll come with me, won't you, son?'

Toby shook his head, his lower lip quivering once again. But no amount of his parents' reassurances convinced him to change his mind. His distress soon grew into uncontrollable sobs.

Once again Beth was afraid they might have to use the pack she had brought.

Tristan ran his hands over his short hair. 'I'll go first.' He looked at Mr Hill. 'You'll come next. Your wife can pass Toby to you while I help her down. We've got to hurry.'

He levered himself through the opening until he could jump down. Mr Hill followed suit.

'It's OK, Toby. See Daddy? I'm going to hand you to him and when I get down, I'll hold you again,' Mrs Hill coaxed.

Toby's sobs lessened, as if he considered this a new and exciting adventure. Once the men were on their feet Mrs Hill passed Toby to his father and accepted Tristan's help until she, too, reached safety.

Tristan reached toward Beth. 'Come on.'

She shook her head. She didn't want to explain how heights bothered her—standing on a ladder's first rung made her knees weak. 'I'm fine. Take Toby to OR. Don't waste time here.'

For a brief second indecision crossed his face. Then, as if he recognized the sense in her suggestion, he nodded. 'I'll send someone back.' His lopsided smile appeared. 'Don't go away.'

She grinned at his inane comment. 'I won't.'

They disappeared from her limited view. Beth sank to

the cool tile floor. With only her thoughts and the blowing exhaust fan for company, she leaned against the wall and prepared to wait. A feeling of deep satisfaction came over her—the same peaceful feeling she'd experienced whenever she'd helped hold off the Grim Reaper. This little patient, in spite of his serious condition and the crucial next twenty-four hours, would be fine. She knew it.

She replayed the past events in her mind. As the scenes unfolded she realized something else—something she'd never thought possible. In spite of the freak mechanical malfunction and in spite of Tristan Lockwood's presence her performance had been perfect. Everything had proceeded as it should have; she hadn't dropped, spilled or tripped over anything. She giggled aloud, her laughter eerie in the silence.

Her professional confidence, at least where Tristan Lockwood was involved, had been restored.

While she was rejoicing over the turn of events Harold—a khaki-uniformed maintenance man in his late fifties—arrived. 'I guess ya do have a problem here.'

Beth scooted closer to the opening. 'You could say that,' she replied without rancor. Nothing could dim her mood, even if she had to sit here all night.

'We heard the buzzer, but figured some kids were just havin' a joke. The repair man was here only yesterday.'

'Maybe so, but something went haywire.'

'I'll say. If you're in a hurry I'll help you through the hole. Isn't far.'

Indecision plagued her. Her ward needed her. 'How long will it take to lower the elevator?'

He opened the panel and studied the wires. 'Hard ta

say. Few minutes, mebbe an hour. 'Pends on what's wrong.' He scratched his scalp. 'May have ta call the company.'

She made up her mind. 'I'll wait five minutes. If you can't fix it by then I'll jump.'

'Suit yerself.'

'Great.' Beth moved to the back. Luckily, less than five minutes later the unit slowly descended. With another jerk it came to stop.

Holding the pack she'd brought along, Beth stepped onto solid ground and fought the urge to kiss the floor. 'Thanks, Harold,' she said.

'S'what I'm here for,' he answered.

Ready to return to her unit, she bypassed the other elevator and walked to the nearest stairwell. The two flights ahead of her seemed infinitely safer than a metal box dangling from a cable.

She strode onto the ward just as the staff began unloading the supper cart. Mary caught sight of her and teased, 'Someone from OR called and told us what happened. Such excitement! And on your first day, too.'

Beth smiled. Tristan had thought of everything. 'Stressful is more like it. I'm taking the stairs for a while, though.'

Mary pulled out two food trays and headed toward a room. 'When we get a chance you can tell me all about it,' she said over her shoulder.

Time passed quickly. Beth distributed meals, poured water and spoonfed a nine-month-old. Then, to relieve Millie's mother, she played one round of the chutes and ladders board game.

At long last a sedated Toby returned from surgery. By

the time Beth and the recovery room nurses had transferred him into bed, rechecked his vital signs and IV line, she was more than ready for a break.

Wanting to spend every moment with Daniel, she drank a can of V-8 juice on her way to the nursery. Once there she scrubbed her hands and threw a plain blue gown over her pediatric smock. Approaching Daniel's incubator, she tied the strings at her nape.

'I wondered if you were coming,' Ann remarked. 'The kiddies keeping you busy?'

'Very.'

'We just received Daniel's latest bilirubin result.'

Hope flared. 'Did it drop?'

Ann shook her head. 'No, but it hasn't risen either.'

'That's some consolation.'

'His bedtime snack is almost ready. Want to do the honors?'

'As if you had to ask,' Beth answered.

Ann delivered a bottle containing a few ounces of warm formula. Beth opened the portholes and raised Daniel to a sitting position, cradling his head and back in her hands. 'Are you hungry, fella?' she asked, thrilled to see his blue eyes open and focus in her direction.

With one hand she held Daniel's upper body. With the other, she brought the nipple to his mouth.

His toothless gums clamped down on the rubber in an instant. He began to suck, grunting with apparent satisfaction.

'My goodness,' Beth exclaimed. 'Greedy little thing, aren't you?'

Ann peeked over her shoulder. 'He's eating very well. If he keeps it up we'll be taking out the IV.'

'Did you hear that, Daniel? Won't it be great to get rid of all those nasty tubes?' Beth said in a low voice. She talked to him the entire time, thrilled to see his gaze lingering on her face. Although she enjoyed caring for him she couldn't wait for the day she could cuddle him next to her heart.

As he swallowed the last drops of milk his eyelids drooped and his jaw grew slack. She pulled the bottle out of his mouth and held him in a more vertical position. Rubbing his back brought the desired results.

'My, what a big burp for such a little guy,' she said. With reluctance she laid him down, careful to place him so that he wouldn't asphyxiate if he brought up any formula. She would never forgive herself if anything happened to him while he was in her care.

From his place at the doorway Tristan leaned against the frame to watch. The Bethany he'd seen with the Hill boy and with Daniel wasn't anything like the Bethany he had observed all those months in ER. This one had a grace and a coolness under fire—traits that other physicians had seen but he hadn't.

Nancy had obviously been right—*he*, with his brusque manner, had contributed to Bethany's ineptitude. He should have realized it himself but he'd been too wrapped up in his own concerns—his own projects, his own hurts—for someone else.

He watched her bend over the incubator. Although her back was to him he could hear her soft, lilting voice. And, to be honest, he enjoyed the gentle sway of her hips as she shifted her stance from time to time. He smiled. It had been a long time since something so elemental had caught his eye.

Although he wouldn't admit it aloud—and couldn't explain why—he *was* drawn to Bethany. Reasons like sympathy, empathy and a newly awakened physical attraction came to mind. A measure of guilt rested on his shoulders, too, in spite of his earlier denial.

Perhaps after he had followed Nancy's advice and apologized life could return to normal. It wouldn't be the same work-centered style he'd thrived on the past few years but, whatever it was, it would be one where thoughts of Bethany wouldn't plague him all hours of the day.

Intent on achieving his objective and regaining his peace of mind, he straightened. With a few long strides he crossed the small room with a plan to put her at ease. His apology would come as a shock after all this time.

'I thought I'd find you here,' he said.

Beth closed the portholes before she glanced at him. 'I'm becoming a creature of habit, I guess.'

'Did you have a long wait to be rescued?'

She grinned. 'Only a few minutes.'

'You should have jumped with us. What if the cable broke and the elevator fell?'

'It didn't.'

'No, but we didn't know that. Besides, you could have been stuck there for hours.'

'I wasn't,' she pointed out. Rubbing her jaw, she added in a reluctant tone, 'I'm afraid of heights. It would have taken too long for me to gather my courage. I couldn't delay Toby's treatment.'

Tristan appeared stunned. 'I never dreamed. . .'

She grinned. 'Don't worry about it. The boy reached OR in time. That's all that matters.'

'Yes, but when I think of what could have happened. . .' He shook his head. 'Things could have gotten tense while we were stuck between floors.'

'But they didn't.'

'Thanks to you.'

A wrinkle appeared on her forehead and between her brows. 'I didn't do anything.'

He shrugged. 'Maybe not directly, but you were invaluable. You kept his mother calm which, in turn, kept Toby relaxed. You had a hemostat in your pocket—I only had spare change.'

She fingered the latch on Daniel's incubator, her face turning pink. 'Daniel finished almost three ounces of formula tonight.'

Amused by her change of subject, Tristan followed her lead. Apparently she had a hard time accepting compliments. He'd have to remember that.

'He is doing very well,' he agreed. 'I wouldn't be surprised if we move him to a regular bassinet before the week's over.'

The gold flecks in her eyes seemed to brighten. 'Really?'

He nodded. The dark circles under her eyes prompted his next question. 'I wonder, though, how you're doing?'

Beth fidgeted, once again avoiding his gaze. 'I'm fine.'

Tristan quirked one eyebrow in disbelief.

She rubbed her temples. 'There are so many things to deal with—like car insurance, health insurance, estate matters. The list is endless. It's overwhelming at times.'

He remembered. He, however, had been lucky—he'd had family to help him. Bethany's friends, through no fault of their own, had left her to cope alone.

Her voice softened. 'Then there's Daniel.'

He waited, unsure of how to vocalize what needed to be asked. 'Do you still want him?'

'Absolutely.' Her answer was vehement.

'Then may I offer a piece of advice?' At her nod he continued, 'Don't try to handle everything yourself. Lots of people would be willing to help you.'

She pursed her lips, as if she found the idea distasteful.

'Take your car situation, for example. You still don't have one, right?' Without waiting for her to agree, he pressed on. 'You're walking home after work, aren't you?'

Once again her face turned a becoming shade of pink. 'Well, um, actually—'

'Any number of people on this shift would give you a ride. There's Mary and Ann. Even myself.'

'I don't want to impose.'

Suddenly Tristan understood what had put the wary look in her eyes—the wary look he'd noticed long ago. At some time during her childhood she'd been made to feel as if she'd been a burden. No wonder the quartet of friends had endured long after most childish friendships dissolved.

He lowered his voice. 'People won't think less of you because you ask for help.'

Beth met his gaze. 'Old habits die hard.'

How well he understood that cliché. He'd steered clear of emotional entanglements—first out of pain, then out of respect for his wife's memory. 'But they can be put to rest,' he remarked, 'provided you have something good to take their place.'

'I'll keep your advice in mind. Goodnight, Doctor.'

By the time she'd fled around the corner he realized something else. He hadn't apologized.

A slow grin spread across his face. At least he'd taken the first step.

Another ten days hurried by, bringing with them a new month. Beth arrived at the nursery on Saturday morning with her spirits high. Daniel's bilirubin level had dropped, eliminating his sessions under the special light.

The moment she stepped onto the mat outside the unit's entrance she noticed Tristan and several nurses hovering over the incubator. Had something happened? Had he needed CPR? Why hadn't someone called?

Fear set in and she scrubbed her hands in record time. Grabbing the first gown she touched, she thrust her arms through the holes and rushed closer without taking the time to tie it around her neck. 'What's wrong?'

'Look who's here,' the day nurse said, wearing a broad smile.

Puzzled by the woman's happy expression, Beth glanced at Tristan. 'Are you ready for a surprise?' he asked.

She took a peek at Daniel. Then another. 'He doesn't have the catheter *or* the IV,' she exclaimed, finally noticing the obvious.

'As of a few minutes ago he's on his own. We're moving him to the regular nursery,' Tristan said. 'You're just in time for his unveiling.'

Emotion clogged her throat and tears of joy filled her eyes.

Tristan flipped the top latches and lowered one side. He lifted a freshly diapered Daniel while a nurse laid a blanket on the thin mattress. After a few tucks and folds, Tristan cradled the small boy in the crook of one arm. 'Hi, big guy. Someone special is here to see you.'

He grinned at Daniel, then at Beth. His broad smile made him appear younger and more approachable. 'Are you ready to hold him?' he asked.

The moment she'd been waiting for had finally arrived. Unable to find her voice, she bobbed her head up and down.

He passed the tiny bundle into her waiting arms. Beth stared at Daniel who, with his eyes wide, seemed interested in this latest development. She reveled in the feel of his tiny body, his baby-fresh scent, his soft skin. 'Hi, sweetie,' she crooned. 'I'm Beth. I'm going to be your mommy.'

Daniel stuck two fingers into his mouth.

Beth tore her gaze from her soon-to-be son and glanced at the nurses. Their eyes were suspiciously moist. Her attention rested on Tristan, although she spoke to all of them. 'I'm always telling you this, but I can't say it often enough. Thank you.'

CHAPTER SIX

FOR the next few minutes the group hovered around Beth. Finally Tristan cleared his throat. 'We'll leave you two to get acquainted.'

Before he turned away Beth caught him with a look of longing on his face. In that moment, gazing on Daniel, she understood his pain, although she didn't know how to alleviate it.

For the next two hours she talked, sang and whispered nonsense to Daniel. She changed his diaper, fed, burped and rocked him to sleep. Though she knew she should, she couldn't return him to his bassinet. Not yet.

'You'll spoil him, you know,' Margaret, the day nurse, commented in her grandmotherly voice. 'Take my advice. Don't let him get used to being held all the time. You'll create a little tyrant.' Her wrinkled face beamed down at her. 'Ah, but he deserves a little extra TLC to make up for his rough start.'

Beth grinned. 'I think so.' Her stomach rumbled and she noticed that it was well past noon. Although she would have preferred to hold him longer it was time she tackled a few household tasks and sewing projects. She had the weekend off and planned to accomplish a lot.

After checking the apnea monitor in his bed, she laid him in his bassinet as carefully as if he were an irreplaceable treasure. Which, in her eyes, he was.

She dropped her gown into the soiled linen bag and

made her way outdoors. Outside the hospital she took a deep breath, catching a whiff of wood smoke from a nearby house. It was a welcome change to the smell of sickness and disinfectant—the two odors she'd inhaled almost exclusively the past few days. The Indian summer breeze caressed her skin and ruffled a few loose strands of hair which had escaped her barrette.

She thrust her hands in the front pockets of her faded blue jeans and set out for home, enjoying the red and gold leaves on the maple and oak trees lining the sidewalk. Maybe the settlement check for the car would be in today's mail. She hoped so.

She'd need a vehicle next week to handle another nurse's insurance physicals while the woman went to Silver Dollar City on vacation. The work wouldn't be taxing and would take only a few hours a day. It seemed almost wrong to earn such a large sum of money for taking medical histories, a few vital signs and an occasional blood sample, but she was thrilled to have the opportunity.

A horn honked. She glanced in its direction, surprised to see Tristan's familiar black BMW inching down the street.

'How about a lift?' he called through the open passenger window.

With her mood as bright as a shiny penny, she couldn't refuse. 'Sure.' Climbing in, she asked, 'Going home too?'

He nodded, pulling back into the line of traffic. 'Just finished my rounds. I saw you walking and wondered if you'd like to have lunch.'

She'd planned to decline, but his hopeful expression stopped her. This man had done so much for her—for

Daniel, actually—that she couldn't refuse. Mindful of her slim finances, a suggestion popped out of her mouth before she could stop it.

'I have a better idea. A pan of lasagna is baking in my oven even as we speak. You're welcome to join me.'

'Love to.'

His lopsided smile returned, making him appear years younger and much more carefree than the man she was used to working with. If he sent many more of those charming grins her way her heart's immunity wouldn't last. And that, considering her impoverished circumstances and his affluence, would never do.

As he parked on the street she glanced at her home, remembering the last time—the only time—he'd been inside. A sudden wave of shyness replaced her earlier euphoria.

He obviously remembered, too. 'Looks bigger in the daylight,' he commented, striding up the walk beside her.

'I guess.' Suddenly tongue-tied, she quickly unlocked the front door and thrust it open. The scent of garlic and oregano drifted through.

'Smells good,' he commented, following her inside. He shrugged off his windbreaker, revealing a plaid short-sleeved shirt in dark colors that matched his hunter-green chino trousers. His shoulder muscles flexed under the cotton as he hung the jacket on an empty wall peg near the door.

'Thanks.' It was a good thing he usually hid his body underneath white coats and scrub suits, she thought. Any female past puberty would be distracted.

Pushing the sleeves of her cream-colored turtleneck sweater past her elbows, she mentally regrouped. 'By the time I've tossed a salad our lunch should be ready. Have a seat in the living room. I'll only be a minute.' Without waiting to see if he followed her instructions, she fled into the relative safety of her kitchen.

Once again a three-letter word kept coming to her mind—why? Why was he here?

With the refrigerator door open, she bent over to yank on the vegetable crisper drawer and pull out half of a head of lettuce, a tomato and a cucumber. Thank goodness she'd given in to impulse and splurged on those last two items. Her salads usually consisted of unadulterated head lettuce.

She stood up and pivoted, plowing right into Tristan's broad chest.

He grabbed her shoulders to steady her and grinned. 'Thought you could use some help. Salads are my specialty.' He held up his hands as if he'd just completed a surgical scrub. 'Have to have the right technique, you know.'

Unbidden, her gaze fell to his long, lean fingers. Unbidden, the memory of him caressing her cheek returned with full force—a memory that expanded with lightning speed to other delightful pursuits. . . She shivered. 'Hmm, sure.'

Beth dropped the produce on the counter and hunted for utensils while he washed his hands. Her clear etched-glass bowl with its chipped rim—courtesy of a garage sale—and an old paring knife joined the vegetables. The idea of serving Tristan Lockwood with flawed dishes made her wish she could rescind her invitation. At least she had a set of four matching plates, courtesy of another yard sale bargain.

Before she'd realized it she heard herself apologizing. 'Lunch won't be as fancy as what you're used—'

His fingers curled around her shoulder. 'Don't. Everything is perfect. Besides, the best food in the world is tasteless if you aren't in the right company. Everything is fine.' He emphasized his last words.

She nodded, her smile weak.

'What do you want me to do?' he asked.

Tell me why you've changed. Instead, she answered, 'The lettuce, please.'

'You got it.' He began tearing the leaves into bite-sized pieces.

While he worked Beth found two pastel place-mats and arranged their matching napkins alongside the plates. A question burned in her mind, the same question she'd wanted to ask before and had lacked the courage to do so. She nibbled on her lower lip.

'You're probably wondering why I'm here,' he said in an offhand manner.

Beth stopped short, amazed by his perception. Unable to deny her interest, especially since he'd brought up the subject, she turned to face him. 'Yes. Yes, I am.'

Tristan tossed the last chunk into the bowl and picked up the cucumber. 'I owe you an apology.'

She dropped her jaw, then snapped it closed. 'For what?'

He sliced in a steady rhythm. 'I misjudged you long ago. As a result, I've never given you a fair chance.'

'What made you change your mind?'

He shrugged. 'A combination of things. Toby, Daniel, other doctors.'

'You discussed me with other doctors?' She raised her voice, horrified at the idea.

'Actually, it was only Dr Sullivan. And in the most general terms,' he said defensively, now quartering the tomato. 'I wanted his opinion as he had more experience working with you than I did. I had my patients to consider.'

Beth fell silent, unsure if she should be flattered or offended by his attention. It reminded her of too many times when schoolmates had befriended her in order to discover something new to send around the gossip mill. Out of lifelong habit, she hid her turmoil behind a stoic face. Only her shaking hands betrayed her as she turned the faucet on full blast to rinse the sink. Another hard twist to shut off the water brought a cry of protest from the pipes.

As if sensing her displeasure, he added, 'I wasn't checking up on you. I made a judgmental error and I'm trying to correct it. Clear the air, so to speak.' He dumped the vegetables onto the shredded lettuce.

His out-of-character politeness now made sense. 'It wasn't necessary.'

'Yes, it was.'

His actions were commendable. Even after revising a faulty first impression, few people would have confessed to having one in the first place. Unless, of course, the wronged party's opinion was valued. Her spirits lifted.

'I don't want any unfinished business between us,' Tristan added. 'From past experience, I know how it eventually interferes with a work relationship.'

The faint hope that he might have a more personal motivation died a swift and painful death. Skirting him, she grabbed the stainless-steel flatware from the drawer and placed the eating utensils around the plates with a precision guaranteed to make Emily Post proud.

'Problems?' she asked, pretending nonchalance. 'We're both professionals. We can shelve our differences should any develop. For the sake of our patients.'

He grabbed her elbow. 'That's what I'm talking about. I don't want to just "shelve" anything. I want issues discussed, dealt with then forgotten.'

His voice lowered. 'People who can relax together—be friends—make for a well-functioning team. I want that, not only because we don't need the additional stress but because of the benefits it gives my—our—patients.'

'You're right,' she said, her voice strangely quiet. 'What's happened in the past is over. Apology accepted.' Platonic friendship was better than the silent war they'd fought this past year. Regardless of her fantasy, she had one consolation—she had proved her abilities, her competence.

Tristan's smile shone out and his tense shoulders slumped with his deep breath.

She rested one arm along the back of a scarred kitchen chair, hardly noticing the wobble caused by its uneven wooden leg in her attempt to play the new role he'd thrust upon her. 'I'll probably still drop things once in a while,' she warned. 'It happens when I'm nervous.'

'Then I'll have to make sure you don't get jittery,' he declared, the corners of his eyes crinkling. He sniffed the air. 'Now that we have the serious stuff out of the way can we eat?' His boyish smile was infectious.

'Certainly. As soon as you pour the iced tea.' While he did so Beth couldn't keep herself from commenting on his expertise. 'You're handy in the kitchen, aren't you?'

He grinned. 'Purely out of self-preservation. After Elise died I brushed off my old medical school recipes. Eating out—eating alone—grows old fast.'

Her name had been Elise. She'd never heard it mentioned before. Beth envisioned a tall, poised young woman with a beauty to match her name.

Using hotpads Ellen had crocheted she pulled the pan out of the oven. She sliced Tristan a large piece of lasagna, struggling not to notice how it didn't look as meaty or cheesy as the picture on the pasta box. With only half the filling ingredients, she couldn't expect it to.

Tristan took his first bite. 'Delicious.'

Warming under his praise, she diverted the subject. 'Why did you decide to upgrade Mercer's nursery?'

His expression became thoughtful. 'As you know, my wife died four years ago. She was six months pregnant with our first child. She'd wanted to visit her grandmother in Seattle, but hadn't wanted to fly. The train seemed much safer, in her eyes, even though it meant travelling for several more days.'

He drew a deep breath. 'For some reason, about halfway there—in the middle of nowhere—the track gave way and the train derailed. My wife and several others were critically injured. Unfortunately, the closest town's hospital facilities had been downgraded for lack of a physician. The staff only handled minor emergencies.

'To make a long story short, both she and our son died before a medical helicopter could arrive. I wanted to prevent a similar situation from happening here.'

Beth hated to think of how Ellen's situation might have ended if not for his decision. She laid her hand on his. 'Ellen and Daniel reminded you of them.'

Tristan speared another square of pasta on his fork. 'It was like I was in the middle of the same nightmare but this time I saw it from a different viewpoint. We're lucky Daniel is a tough little guy. We could have easily lost him the night of the ice storm.'

Beth shuddered. She didn't want to think about it.

'All of my patients are important to me. I try not to get emotionally attached but Daniel is special.'

'I'm prejudiced, of course, but I agree,' she replied.

For a fleeting moment she wondered where Tristan's interests lay. With her—or with Daniel? She pushed aside the unwelcome thought.

'Do you need anything for Daniel?' he asked. 'You'll be bringing him home soon.'

'Thanks to Ellen's advance planning, we're set. I only need to assemble his crib. Once I find the right gadgets for the job, that is.'

'Maybe I can help. I keep a few basic things in my car for emergencies. I also have a nicely outfitted tool chest at home.'

'You're one of those guys who putters in the garage?'

A wide and easy grin spread across his face. 'Yes and no. I did a lot of woodworking with my father as a kid, but medical school ended that. After I started my practice Dad suggested I took it up again—sort of a stress reliever. I started a few projects for Elise and the baby, but. . .' he shrugged and his mouth straightened '. . .I lost interest.'

He didn't need to explain—her intuition supplied the answer. Trying to keep the atmosphere light, she injected a cheery note into her voice. 'Thanks for the offer. I've been wondering how I'd match piece A with hole B.

Unlike my friends, Kirsten and Naomi, I'm not mechanically inclined.'

His smile emerged, like the sun coming out from behind a rain cloud. 'You know all my secrets. Tell me yours. How did you end up in a county-run home?'

Beth toyed with a string of cheese clinging to her plate. 'My father was in the Service. He was killed when his Jeep overturned on some training mission when I was only a baby. My mom had a lot of health problems; she died of pneumonia when I was seven.' She fell silent, reliving the experience of being totally uprooted.

'And then?' he asked softly.

'I lived with my dad's sister until her fiancé gave her an ultimatum. It was either him or me. I was ten when I entered foster care and thirteen when I finally moved into the girls' home.' Tristan frowned and she hurried to minimize the ordeal. She didn't want his pity.

'The group I stayed with was wonderful. Our house parents were very good to us—kept us from becoming complete hellions. I owe them a lot.'

'And your aunt?'

She shrugged. 'I lost contact with her. Just one of those things, I guess.' To keep her maudlin thoughts at bay, she changed the subject. 'How about dessert?'

He patted his stomach. 'No room. Maybe later.'

With the meal over, Tristan disappeared down the hall to inspect the baby bed while Beth stacked the dirty dishes and tidied the otherwise spartan kitchen. Every noise coming from the other room seem magnified, and the tread of his soft-soled loafers on the hardwood floor soon heralded his return.

'I'll run home for my power screwdriver. Now I can

finally use the Christmas present my dad gave me.'

His pocket pager interrupted with its annoying bleep. 'May I use your phone?' he asked.

She pointed to the wall.

Tristan punched a number from memory. A few minutes later his apologetic expression forewarned of bad news. 'I have to drop by the hospital. A possible appendicitis case. I'm sorry. We'll have to assemble the crib later.'

Beth pasted a smile on her face to hide her disappointment and a small measure of skepticism about his return. Although Tristan seemed to take his word seriously, she didn't know him well enough—or trust him—to erase all doubts. Besides, he was a busy pediatrician. He didn't have time to bother himself with mundane tasks.

'No problem. Some other time.'

'I mean it,' he insisted, his gaze as steady and unwavering as the Rock of Gibraltar. 'I'll be back.'

She quirked one eyebrow. 'I'll be here.'

One corner of his mouth turned upward into his easy smile. Before she realized what was happening he'd cupped her face in his hands.

With slow, methodical movements he stroked the boundaries of the red mark along her jaw. She moved to stop him but he shook his head.

She fastened her gaze on his mouth. Anticipating the contact, she parted her lips.

His features came closer until they blurred in her vision. The moment his mouth touched hers she closed her eyes. Tristan's unique scent blended with the spicy aroma of their past meal, creating a fragrance far more tantalizing than any masculine scent on the market.

He deepened his kiss as his arms enfolded her, drawing her to his massive chest. It was as if she were a part, an extension, of him. The buttons on his shirt pressed into her skin, leaving tiny indented circles. His heart thumped beneath her palm, his grunt of satisfaction filled her ears and his breath whispered across her cheek.

Running his hand inside her loose collar, he stroked the column of her neck with a touch so feather-light that it sent shivers down her spine. The pressure of his lips gradually softened until it completely disappeared, leaving only a memory in its wake.

'I *will* be back, Bethany,' he murmured, keeping her tucked against him. 'You know that now, don't you?'

Her voice frozen in her throat, Beth nodded. Waving to him from the door, another question popped into her mind. If he could kiss the socks off a woman in order to keep their work relationship on an even keel how would he kiss the woman he loved?

Beth's trusty sewing machine—a used model purchased during her teenage years—whirred to a stop. With movements testifying to her hours of practice, she cut the threads and removed the finished jumpsuit from under the presser foot. Holding it up, she ran a critical eye over the garment. Daniel would be adorable in her creation with its red and blue appliquéd train on the front.

A light knock at the door caught her attention. She glanced at the kitchen clock, surprised to see that Tristan had arrived earlier than he'd told her.

Her pulse speeded up, excited at the prospect of seeing him. It had been almost twenty-four hours since he'd been called away from her house, and she couldn't think of a better companion for a Sunday afternoon—unless Daniel could be included.

She hurried to the front door and flung it open. To her surprise, someone else stood on the porch. Although she was happy to see her guest, this wasn't the person who'd set her heart racing. Hiding her disappointment behind a bright smile, she greeted her visitor. 'Hi, Katie. What brings you here?'

Katie Alexander held out a plastic tote bag. 'Friends bearing gifts.'

Beth showed her friend to the threadbare and slightly saggy nubby tweed sofa. 'You didn't have to,' she began.

Katie tossed her brown braid over one shoulder. 'Don't thank me yet. My neighbor got bitten by the fall cleaning bug and found this material stuck in a closet.'

She drew the four pieces of sweatshirt fleece fabric out of her bag. 'Her boys are all too old for these cutesy prints so she wanted to give them to someone who might use them. I knew you were a seamstress so I thought I'd see if you were interested. If they don't suit you aren't obligated to take them.'

Beth ran her hand over the soft material covered with designs suitable for little boys—race cars, trucks, tools and balls of all kinds. 'These are wonderful. Perfect, in fact.'

Katie's shoulders slumped and the tension lines around her eyes relaxed. 'I thought about sewing something for Daniel myself, but I'm just learning. He might be in college before I get past the basics.'

Beth laughed. 'No, you won't. I'm not an expert but if you need any help let me know.'

'I appreciate it.' Katie studied her friend. 'I like your

hair. You should wear it that way more often.'

Surprised by the comment as it echoed her three girlhood friends' sentiments, Beth's face warmed. She only created the soft chignon for special occasions and didn't want to admit that today was different from any other. Self-consciously she patted her head. 'Thanks, but it's not practical for work. The only place I go to these days is the hospital.'

'You should try it anyway. By the way, have you heard we're getting not one but *two* ER docs?'

'You're kidding.'

Katie shook her head. 'Nope. The patient satisfaction polls were lousy so Administration finally agreed to add another physician. He's only scheduled part time but we could use another doctor on the weekends.'

The dark-haired woman took a breath and continued. 'Dr Sullivan is leaving sooner than we'd expected, too—the middle of November instead of the first of December.'

'That's less than four weeks. What about his replacement?' Beth asked. 'What's his name?'

'Dr Knox. Apparently he's arriving sooner than originally thought. I hope he's as easy-going as Dr Sullivan. The part-time fellow is a Dr Berkley.' Katie rose to leave. 'Hate to run, but I start my vacation tomorrow. My brother, Gideon, and his wife, Natalie, just had their second baby and I'm on my way to spend a few days spoiling my niece and nephew.' She grinned and a dimple appeared in her cheek.

Beth escorted her to the door. 'Have a nice time. And thanks again.'

A minute later she was alone again, but hopefully not

for long. She hurried into Daniel's future bedroom to add Katie's gift to the pile of fabric waiting for attention.

Beth placed the material on top of the dresser. As she turned away the entire stack shifted. Before she could prevent it, pieces of cloth slipped to the floor.

A sharp crash followed. Her heart heavy, she saw Ellen's jewelry box with its lid open and its previously organized contents scattered haphazardly around her feet.

She gathered the jewelry, grateful that nothing appeared to be broken. Sinking onto the double bed, she began the task of sorting.

Little by little she brought order out of chaos. When she came to her friend's charm bracelet she allowed herself to admire it one more time. The trinkets dangling from the silver bracelet possessed more sentimental than monetary value.

One by one she reminisced at the milestones each piece marked. She remembered giving Ellen the tiny Washington Monument—a souvenir of Beth's trip. There was a small typewriter, given by their business teacher for achieving the highest speed in the class, crossed tennis rackets for making the team. And, finally, a gold key.

The significance hit her at once. Could this be the same key needed to open Ellen's keepsake chest? Without another thought, she retrieved the box from its hiding place in the bottom drawer. Holding it on her lap, she noticed that the size of the hole seemed appropriate.

She inserted the tiny piece of metal and twisted. The click of success echoed in the quiet room, but she refrained from lifting the lid. Curiosity urged her to proceed but caution held her back. Yet if something inside pertained to Daniel. . .

Taking a deep breath and drawing comfort from her friend's residual wildflower fragrance, she raised the lid.

The smell of roses burst forth like a genie out of a bottle. Beth carefully removed a dried corsage, lying on top of a sheaf of envelopes. Two silver dollars, minted near the turn of the century, rested underneath the papers.

She flipped through the letters, finding a few official-looking papers from various insurance companies. Ellen's birth certificate, her parents' death certificates and her school diploma came next.

At the very bottom of the stack were three plain white envelopes. Each was addressed to Ellen in the same masculine hand but lacked a return label. Even the inked postmarks were smudged, as if they'd been wet at one time.

Without removing the contents, she knew who had written them. Daniel's father.

CHAPTER SEVEN

BETH set the correspondence aside, along with the insurance documents, and carefully replaced Ellen's treasures in the box.

The full gamut of emotions passed through her as she locked the chest, tucked it back in the bottom drawer and laid the charm bracelet in its soft nest inside the jewelry case.

She'd never liked unanswered questions. On the surface she was glad that the mystery of Ellen's secret lover would soon be solved.

At the same time, however, fear gripped her in its icy tentacles. Legally this man had more rights to Daniel than she did.

If Ellen had loved this man, and Beth was certain that she had, only something drastic or irrevocable would have kept them apart.

She also rejected the idea of Daniel's father's early demise. No, the man was still alive for Ellen to avoid the topic so faithfully even with her closest friends.

Yet if he possessed some character flaw that had sent Ellen fleeing from him his name was best forgotten.

Beth stared at the envelopes for several minutes, trying to decide her course of action. Should she risk discovering Daniel's father? Or should she destroy the letters unread—pretend they had never existed?

One thing was certain: she'd have to live with her decision for the rest of her life.

Stiffening her spine and shoulders, she lifted the flap of the top envelope and pulled out the single page. Uncomfortable at the idea of reading someone else's love notes, she scanned the contents to reach the signature block.

A scrawled 'J.D.' appeared at the bottom.

Beth opened the others. The writer had signed every one with his initials.

She arranged the pages in chronological order and began to read, this time in more depth. Combining the information she'd gleaned with her personal knowledge of Ellen's activities, she pieced together a picture of the ill-fated couple's relationship by the end of the last letter.

Ellen had met J.D. while in Chicago for a medical records seminar. After she'd returned home to Kansas City they'd carried on a long-distance romance which, from J.D.'s tone, hadn't been particularly satisfying. He'd apparently had something permanent in mind since he'd written of plans for a family meeting.

Still clutching the papers, Beth lowered her hands to her lap. She had more questions than ever, with fewer answers than before. J.D. had lived in Chicago six months ago, and possibly still did. He was an articulate man, sharing Ellen's interest in medicine. A pharmacist, she surmised from his paragraph explaining the effects of tobramycin on the body. He couldn't be a physician—his handwriting was too legible.

Deep in thought, Beth refolded the pages along their original creases. Intense relief burst into her soul. The man's identity remained unknown—he couldn't take

Daniel away from her. Her tension drained away and she slumped as a slow breath passed through her lips. Closing her eyes, she whispered her thanks to the empty room.

A brisk pounding on the front door broke through her maelstrom of thoughts. Realizing that it must be Tristan, she jumped to her feet and stuffed the letters into the top dresser drawer. Smoothing a few loose tendrils of her hair back into its soft knot, she hurried to greet him.

Her heart fluttered with excitement and she quickly tamped down the feeling. One-sided infatuations spelled disaster and she didn't have the stamina to cope with another tragedy. Tristan had only offered his friendship because he wanted them to work together amicably. She would do well to remember that.

Standing on the cement porch with his red tool chest in hand, Tristan fought his own tremor of heart-pounding anticipation. He was only here to build a rapport, a camaraderie between team members, using Daniel and their shared experience of losing someone dear as the foundation. The attraction he felt was simply a physical response to his empathy. He needed to remember that.

In spite of his resolve, the sight of her on the opposite side of the aluminum storm door caused his mouth to curve into a face-splitting smile.

'I see you're ready to work,' Beth said, pointing to his equipment as she welcomed him inside. She held out her hand for his windbreaker, and he handed it over.

'You bet. Just lead the way.' He sniffed the air, recognizing a lingering spicy aroma. 'Something smells good.'

'I made banana nut bread. For afterwards.'

'My favorite.' He grinned. 'Actually, I like any kind

of home-baked food. I cook, but bakery goods are beyond my scope. If my mom and sister don't take pity and give me a handout I rely on the store's offerings.'

'Hinting?' she asked, laughter in her voice.

'Would it do any good?'

'Maybe.'

He followed Beth around the corner and into what would soon be Daniel's room.

'Here are the instructions.' She handed him a small booklet.

As he began to read Tristan marveled at how different she looked with her new hairstyle. The few wisps hanging around her face softened her features and gave her a more carefree appearance.

He wondered how many people in the hospital realized how beautiful Beth was. After seeing her today, he thought that the phrase 'diamond in the rough' described her perfectly. If many eligible males had Tristan's good fortune she'd have a steady stream of interested men parading by. Good thing she was somewhat isolated in Pediatrics.

His attention fell to her chin. Once again she wore something with a high collar, this time a cowl-necked sweater. He tried to picture her as he'd seen her on other occasions, struggling to remember a time when she hadn't worn something concealing. Failing, he knew that it was because of her port-wine stain. Well aware of people's cruelty, his anger surged. He'd like to have a few words with the persons responsible for her self-consciousness. He frowned.

'Are we missing a piece?' she asked.

Tristan blinked, composing his features. 'No, just thinking.'

'Oh.' In the next breath she asked, 'How did your appendicitis case turn out?'

'Fine. The eleven-year-old had generalized abdominal pain, some nausea but no vomiting. Her CBC was unremarkable so we kept her for a few hours' observation.'

'What about a sonogram?'

'Didn't tell us anything conclusive. The soreness seemed to go away and her temp was normal so the surgeon agreed to send her home.' He shrugged. 'She may be back. Hand me the pliers, please. Top compartment.'

Beth rummaged around for the requested tool before she chose one and held it up for view. 'Is this what you're looking for?'

'Yeah.' Using the pliers to hold the metal washer steady, Tristan turned the screw joining the headboard to the mattress frame. Kneeling on the floor next to him, Bethany's floral scent wafted toward him with each movement.

'You're an old hand at this,' she remarked, holding the two pieces of wood together.

'I've assembled a few things before.' He paused. 'The last piece was our baby crib.' He'd had an assistant then, too—Elise.

He heard a gasp and saw her cheeks tinged with pink. No doubt she regretted accepting his help, afraid that she'd brought back bittersweet memories. She had, but they were more sweet than bitter. 'Don't be upset,' he murmured. 'You didn't know. I'm OK.'

She stared into his eyes. Then, as if certain that he

spoke the truth, a tentative smile hovered on her mouth and she nodded.

Although he ached to walk his fingers across her full lips he only allowed his gaze to trace the softness.

Reality set in with the abruptness of a sonic boom. He was supposed to cultivate an amicable relationship, not a romantic one. He cleared his throat and grabbed another bolt. 'I think we're ready to connect the other side.'

The highly charged moment passed. Without further prompting, she picked up the other board and held it in place.

For the next few minutes Tristan concentrated on his task, filling the silence with the whir of his power screwdriver. Conversation ebbed, except for an occasional 'Hold that, please,' interspersed with, 'Are there any more bolts?'

Finally, he stood back to survey his handiwork, conscious of Beth's nearness. 'Looks good.' He shook the frame, satisfied that it held firm. 'Daniel can bounce all he likes. It should hold.'

Beth tucked a loose lock of hair behind one ear. 'Thanks. I couldn't have done it on my own.'

He glanced around the room. 'I have a baby swing and a play-pen. You're welcome to them. They'll never be used—my nieces and nephews are past the age.'

Her eyes grew wide. 'But you might want them someday.'

'I doubt it.'

'What if you get married again?'

Tristan shook his head. Bending down, he replaced his tools in the chest and snapped the lid closed. 'Elise and I had a very special relationship. Even if it were possible to love another woman the same way, I won't. I buried one wife and child. I can't do it again.'

The silence grew deafening as Beth ran her hand along the curves of the headboard. After a long pause she drew a deep breath. 'In any case, I appreciate your offer but, as you can see, I don't have the space.'

He rose. 'If you should change your mind. . .'

'I'll let you know.' Beth's face brightened. 'I'm thirsty. How about you?'

He gave her a lazy grin. 'I thought you'd never ask.'

As he ate the nut bread and drank his unsweetened iced tea while sitting on her threadbare sofa he wondered how to break his news about Daniel. Second-guessing her reaction, he'd debated saying nothing until the last moment. But he quickly rejected that notion, knowing that Bethany would never forgive him. Although he couldn't say why, he didn't want her to hold any resentment against him.

No, he needed to give her the facts, along with a few days to grow accustomed to the situation.

He washed down the remnants of his second slice and wiped his mouth on a cloth napkin. Leaning against the cushions, he ran his arm along the top of the divan.

'I'm really proud of Daniel's progress,' he began.

'Isn't it wonderful? I saw him this morning and it seems like he improves daily.'

'He does. He'll be ready to leave the hospital soon.' Tristan monitored her expression.

'Really? I can't wait. When?'

'A few days. Wednesday or Thursday.'

Horror erased her joyful countenance at the exact second she pieced the dates together on her mental calendar. 'But our court hearing isn't until a week from Tuesday.'

'I know.'

'You know?' She jumped to her feet. 'How?'

'I spoke with Edith White before I came over.' He watched her pace the floor. 'I had to. Legally, Daniel is a ward of the court.'

'I understand that.' Beth crossed her arms and rubbed them as if she were cold. 'She won't let me have him early, will she?'

He had suggested it but Edith hadn't been receptive. Tristan leaned forward, resting his forearms on his knees. 'No.'

'She's going to make him go to foster care, isn't she?'

The pain in her eyes nearly undid him. He swallowed, wishing he'd been more persuasive. Unfortunately Edith White was too strong-willed to be swayed. Fearing that he might hurt Beth's cause if he persisted, he'd let the subject drop. 'I'm afraid so.'

Beth rubbed her neck. 'Isn't there anything you can do? Stall his discharge until the hearing?'

'If he continues to progress I'll be hard pressed to keep him until Thursday. The quality assurance folks monitor the lengths of hospital stays. I can't keep Daniel without a sound medical reason.'

Beth wandered to the window. Holding the curtain aside, she stared into the street and said nothing.

God, she was taking this harder than he'd expected. He moved behind her. Taking her shoulders in his large hands, he pulled her against his chest, spoon fashion, and rested his chin on top of her head. Her apple-scented shampoo filled his nostrils.

'Ms White said she'd arrange for you to meet the foster parents,' he said.

Holding her was like holding a board. Tristan wrapped his arms around her. He continued, 'You'll be able to visit Daniel every day. She understands your concern and has been working to find the best place for him.'

'I'll bet.'

He ignored her sarcasm. 'The couple she has in mind have had other babies with problems. They've had an infant with cystic fibrosis, one with a cleft palate, one with—'

'If that's supposed to make me feel better it's not working.'

Her flat tone bothered him. 'It's only for a few days. Daniel will be fine.'

'Promise?' She twisted in his arms to face him. 'Can you promise that absolutely nothing will happen to him?'

'I want to but I can't, any more than I can make the same promise for you.'

'Surely she could bend the rules.'

'Some people will, others won't. Edith White falls into the second category.'

'They love their power, don't they?' Her cynicism was unmistakable.

Although he agreed that the sentence described Edith, he sensed that she referred to the Social Services department in general. 'Some do. Some don't.'

Suddenly she melted against his chest. 'Daniel belongs with me, Tristan,' she sobbed. 'With *me*. Not someone who doesn't love him.'

'And you'll get him,' he soothed, struggling with a lump in his throat. Beth's experience must have been horrible for her to react with such vehemence after all these years. 'Just be patient.'

Her tears flowed in torrents. He held her close, stroking her soft hair. If only he could do more than offer comfort.

Several minutes later Beth wiped her tear-streaked face with her hands and stepped out of Tristan's embrace. 'I turn into a regular water-fountain around you. Sorry about that.'

'I don't mind.' He tipped her chin up so that their eyes met. 'Want to talk about it?'

She twisted her mouth into a tiny smile. 'Not really, but I suppose I should.'

He let her go, then sat next to her on the sofa.

Beth clasped her hands together on her lap. 'I was in foster care before I went to the Home where I met Ellen. The people I lived with were licensed to have five children. They had two boys, five and seven, a baby about a year old and myself. Why they agreed to keep five of us I'll never know. We had it drilled into us how much trouble we were.

'Anyway, the police brought a twelve-year-old retarded boy one night because they had no other place to take him. Henry was supposed to go to another home the next morning.'

She fell silent. 'Before they arrived our foster mother went to the store for cigarettes. Henry went into the baby's room. I guess he wanted to play with little Charlie, and couldn't understand why he didn't wake up. He picked him up and threw him against the wall. Broke Charlie's neck. It was horrible.'

Her hands balled into fists. 'I tried to stop him but Henry was bigger and stronger than I was. I know he didn't hurt him out of meanness—' She shook her head. 'That woman should never have left us alone.'

'No, she shouldn't have.'

'We all left the same day.' Her voice rose. 'Daniel doesn't deserve to be in a place like that. I don't care if it's only for a few hours. It's too long.'

He didn't want to get involved and yet he couldn't help himself. 'I don't know how much good I can do, but I'll talk to Ms White again.'

Hope flared in her eyes. 'You will?'

He took her hands in his and gently pried her fingers loose from each other. 'I can't promise success but I'll do my best.'

Beth cinched the belt on her black dress trousers another notch and studied her face in the mirror. Even to her, her eyes looked tired, staring out above dark circles. She dabbed on more concealer. Sleep hadn't come easily, if at all, the past few nights. Ever since Tristan had mentioned Daniel's imminent discharge she had battled her memories and it had taken its toll.

And now, today, the moment she'd been dreading since Sunday would arrive. Daniel was going to a foster home.

This week's routine had been demanding. Each morning she'd given insurance physicals for several hours. Then she'd rushed home to change, before dashing to the nursery. For the next few hours, until her shift began, she'd cared for Daniel. After work she'd driven home in her newly acquired, albeit used, Pontiac Sunbird, watched television or read until her eyelids drooped, then crawled into bed. A few hours later the cycle had repeated itself.

Beth hurried to the hospital, anxious to spend as much time as possible with Daniel before he left. She arrived in time for his morning bath.

As soon as she lowered him into the basin a stream of fluid shot upwards like a geyser. She quickly tossed a washcloth over his private parts. His surprise over his new and exciting ability was priceless. 'Daniel,' she scolded him without real emphasis.

'He got you, didn't he?' Tristan chuckled as he joined her. 'Typical little boy. You'll have to be quicker, Mom.'

'I guess so.' She soaped and rinsed him, reveling in the fresh baby scent. 'Don't you feel better now?' she chattered. 'All nice and clean.'

Tristan handed her a towel. 'I'm sorry Ms White wouldn't budge,' he said.

Beth dried Daniel, then expertly taped on a disposable diaper. 'You tried. I appreciate the effort.'

She dressed him in a sleeper Ellen had purchased. It hung on his tiny frame but he'd soon fill it out. This time she wrapped him in a lightweight blanket of her own since the hospital linens had to remain. Once he was snug she cradled him in the crook of her arm and settled in a rocking chair to feed him.

Daniel had barely taken two swallows when Edith White and another well-dressed woman walked into the anteroom.

Beth stiffened. 'I thought they weren't coming for a few hours,' she ground out.

'There's been a change in plans.' Tristan's face held an apologetic expression. 'Edith called me about thirty minutes ago. She has to leave town unexpectedly so she wants to see Daniel settled beforehand.'

Beth bit her lip until she tasted blood. Deep in her misery, she didn't return Edith's breezy smile. Instead she longed to run out of the building with Daniel and hide him until Tuesday, but she squelched the urge.

'Hello, Ms Trahern,' Edith said. She bent over to peek at Daniel. He eyed her as his mouth worked the nipple. 'Fine-looking boy.'

Edith straightened and introduced Karen Johnson. 'I'm sure you have special instructions, don't you, Doctor?'

'Yes, I do.'

Keeping her gaze fixed on Daniel, Beth listened to Tristan as he discussed medication, the monitoring system for Daniel's bed and a multitude of other concerns. She consoled herself with his detailed instructions, somewhat relieved that Karen paid close attention.

His quick review of CPR made Beth realize something important. Tristan wasn't as nonchalant about the situation as he appeared. He, too, must have had doubts that needed satisfying. 'If you have any questions or concerns, day or night, call me,' he commanded.

Edith glanced at her watch. 'I must leave this very minute. Can you handle our boy?' she asked Karen.

Karen nodded. 'No problem.'

Daniel steadily drained his bottle. When he couldn't suck out another drop Beth knew that the moment had come. Lifting him to her shoulder, she rubbed his back until he burped.

Steeling herself for the task ahead, she rose.

Karen handed her a piece of paper. 'Here's our address

and phone number. Anytime you want to call or stop by, feel free.'

Beth shoved the note into her pants pocket. 'Thanks.'

Karen touched her arm. 'I only keep one infant at a time so he'll get plenty of attention.'

Beth couldn't reply. With her backbone stiff, she pointed to a diaper bag next to his bassinet. 'There are his things.' She lowered him to the crook of her arm. 'Be good, Daniel.'

Fighting back the tears collecting in her eyes, she handed him to Karen. Her composure rapidly disintegrated. She rushed from the nursery, ignoring Tristan's shout as she brushed past a surprised Margaret.

She speed-walked through the hospital corridors, breaking into a jog near the entrance.

Tristan caught up with her before she slid into her car. He grabbed her wrist. 'Are you OK?'

Beth faced him, her eyes burning. 'What do you think?'

He fell silent.

'Please, Tristan. Just let me go home,' she begged. 'I have to work this out myself.'

His gaze didn't waver. Finally, as if he understood, he released his hold. 'I'll see you later. Try to relax.'

Once at home she tried to follow his advice, but she couldn't. She cleaned her house from top to bottom, dusting and scrubbing until even the dust motes had fled in terror.

She was more than happy to report to Peds later that day, anxious for nursing duties capable of dispelling her worrisome thoughts. One of her patients—the eleven-year-old girl who'd interrupted her afternoon with

Tristan—garnered her attention the minute the shift report ended.

'It hurts really bad, Beth.' Lying in a fetal position, Rachel Robins pressed a hand to the right side of her abdomen.

Beth approached the bed, acknowledging the girl's parents with a brief nod. 'Is it worse than before?' she asked. Rachel had arrived early that morning with abdominal pain and had been readmitted for observation.

Rachel nodded, a single tear slipping out from under her closed eyelids. 'I have to throw up.'

Beth handed her an emesis basin. Clutching it like a lifeline, Rachel decided that she wasn't ready to use it.

To Beth's relief, Tristan entered the room. 'And how is my prettiest patient?'

'Not too good.' Rachel groaned.

'May I take a look?' he asked.

Beth moved to the opposite side of the bed. Tristan moved the blankets and Rachel's nightgown out of the way while Beth held her hand.

He pressed down. 'Does this hurt?'

'Some.'

'I want you to do something for me. Try to cough. Then see if you can put your finger on the spot where it hurts the worst.'

Rachel obliged, pointing to the classic area in her lower right abdomen.

He glanced at Beth. 'Have the CBC results come back?'

'The white cell count is eleven thousand. Her neutrophil count is seventy per cent.' She knew that the elevated white count and the increased percentage of cells involved in fighting a bacterial infection confirmed his unspoken diagnosis.

'Well, my dear, it looks as if you'll leave this time without your appendix,' Tristan remarked. 'Don't worry. It will be over soon.'

'Good,' the youngster replied.

Tristan beckoned the parents into the hallway. 'You'll need to sign a consent form before we take her to surgery. The sooner we remove her appendix the better. I don't want to risk it rupturing.'

Beth hurried to the phone to make the arrangements. Before long she was ready to prep Rachel for surgery.

'Let's get you into one of these hospital gowns,' Beth told her. 'We don't want anything to happen to your pretty nightie.' She sponge-bathed her, shaved her abdomen, recorded her vital signs and administered a sedative.

By the time Beth was finished a surgical nurse had arrived to wheel their young patient away. She helped the other nurse transfer Rachel to the gurney. 'Bye, Rachel. I'll see you when you get back.'

The moment they were gone Beth prepared the bed for Rachel's return, setting up the IV pole and other equipment which might be necessary.

By the time she was satisfied with her work the meal cart arrived.

'See if you can get Michael to eat,' Mary requested. 'The day staff said he refused.'

Beth considered her options. 'He's been in traction for a long time. Maybe he's bored and needs to see a few new faces.'

'It's worth a try,' Mary said.

Beth enlisted the help of two other boys, both seven,

on the unit. Entering Michael's room, she spoke with enthusiasm. 'I've brought some company.'

With his leg in Russell traction for a fractured femur, Michael turned his head to watch John and Cody wheel their chairs close to his bed.

'Hi,' the two boys echoed. 'What happened to you?'

'A car hit me when I was on my bike.'

'Michael was lucky—he could have been hurt a lot worse,' Beth said. 'He likes to fish. He even has a pond behind his house.'

'Wow!' With the ice broken, they chattered about digging worms while they ate their meat loaf and jello.

Beth smiled, pleased to see the five-year-old taking a few bites. By the time their conversation turned to the best method of catching toads he was eating with gusto.

An hour later her boss found her. 'Time for a break,' Mary stated. 'Get something to eat, too. You look as if you'll blow away.'

Opting to stay on the ward, Beth prepared a cup of hot chocolate in the kitchenette. Before the marshmallows had melted an apologetic Mary asked her to handle a new admission. Beth hurried to prepare another croup tent, bringing the number of respiratory cases on the unit to six.

The remaining hours of her shift passed swiftly. Right before her reinforcements arrived the elevator doors whooshed open, relinquishing Rachel Robins, Dr Lockwood and two recovery room nurses.

They soon transferred a groggy Rachel to her regular bed. Beth took her vital signs, unable to ignore the low drone of Tristan's voice as he talked with the girl's parents. Satisfied with Rachel's stable condition, she left the room.

Tristan caught up with her in the hallway. 'How are you doing?'

She knew he wasn't referring to the evening's hectic pace. 'I'm fine.'

'Have you eaten?'

'I've had my supper break.'

'That's not what I asked. Have you eaten?'

She warmed under his piercing study.

'I thought not.' He shook his head. 'You can't function on empty, Bethany.'

'I know, but—'

'You owe it to Daniel to take care of yourself,' he said bluntly. 'He doesn't have anyone else.'

His censure struck home. She was being foolish, allowing her worries to overtake her good sense. 'You're right.'

His lopsided smile appeared. 'The next few days will go quickly. You'll see.'

Beth hoped so.

CHAPTER EIGHT

TUESDAY, October 20th would be etched in Beth's mind for ever.

Striding through the courthouse's hallowed halls, she gripped her shoulder-bag until her knuckles ached. Excited over Daniel's homecoming, her heart beat in rhythm to the butterflies dancing in her stomach.

Tristan grabbed her elbow to stop her. 'Where's the fire?'

She grinned. 'I guess I'm a little eager.'

'We have plenty of time,' he advised. He peered into her face. 'You're looking more rested. Sleeping better?'

'Better than I ever thought I would. I visited Daniel every day,' she said slowly. 'The Johnsons doted on him, treating him like he was their very own. I couldn't believe it. Words can't describe my relief.'

He touched the tip of her nose. 'Didn't I tell you not to worry? Next time you'll follow doctor's orders.'

She snapped a salute. 'Yes, sir.'

Tristan chuckled. 'Come on. I see Mitch Adams.'

Struck by nervous tension, Beth slipped her hand into Tristan's. Comforted by his presence, she walked forward. 'I appreciate your coming with me today. I hope I didn't ruin your schedule.'

'No. My receptionist juggled a few appointments. I'll catch up on the rest later.'

''Morning, Beth,' Mitch called out. His dark hair,

accented by silver-streaked temples, went well with his crisp heather-gray pinstripe suit. His tall, self-assured bearing reminded her of Tristan. Beth applauded her luck in securing such a distinguished-looking attorney.

'Hey, Tris, what brings you here?' He quirked one eyebrow at their intertwined fingers. Beth dropped her hand. 'Lending moral support, perhaps?'

'You're right.'

Mitch clapped him on the shoulder and winked. 'Whatever you say, buddy.' He turned to Beth. 'Any last-minute regrets?'

'Not a one,' she declared, holding her gaze steady.

'Then as soon as the others arrive—' Mitch interrupted himself. 'Looks like they're here.'

Edith White, Karen Johnson and Judge Winters approached. Beth had eyes only for the baby carrier hanging from Karen's hand.

'Hello, everyone,' Edith said briskly.

The judge didn't meet Beth's expectations of an aged and experienced member of the bench. His sandy-colored hair was slicked back and the only grooves in his face were the crow's-feet near his eyes. He couldn't have passed the forty-five mark. 'Are we ready?' he asked.

The bundle of blankets wiggled and a little grunt of protest came from underneath. Karen rearranged the cover, which had fallen over Daniel's face. 'I think *he* is.'

Judge Winters laughed. 'Then let's not make him wait any longer.'

Everyone sat around a huge conference table. Even with the relaxed atmosphere, Beth's stomach tensed into knots. This was the first step in her bid to adopt Daniel. According to Mitch, nothing stood in her way but Beth knew how quickly a situation could turn for the worse.

While the judge reviewed the folder of documents supplied by Edith White, Beth once again slipped her hand into Tristan's. He leaned closer in his chair, his shoulder touching hers. The slight contact calmed her unsteady nerves.

She stole a glance at his profile, grateful for his presence. For a few seconds she entertained a fantasy that they were a couple and that Daniel would be *theirs* and not just hers.

Judge Winters rested his elbows on the table and steepled his fingers. 'I see no reason why Ms Trahern can't be granted temporary guardianship of Daniel McGraw,' he began.

Beth's shoulders sagged in relief.

'Ms White's staff may proceed with a home study since you are also requesting permanent custody. It will take some time to finalize everything, you realize. In addition, the court has to make every effort to find the father. There have been too many overturned adoptions. I don't want this to be one of them.'

'I understand,' Beth said.

'Do you have any idea who or where the father might be?'

Apprehensively she thought of the letters. She had so little information that it hardly seemed worth mentioning. Chicago, the initials J.D. and a medical background were her only clues. But she couldn't divulge those yet. Naomi and Kirsten, with their hospital contacts, planned to do some sleuthing among the many medical facilities in the metropolis.

She tamped down a sliver of guilt. They couldn't let

Daniel into this man's clutches if Ellen had felt it necessary to escape them herself.

Taking a deep breath, Beth said, 'No. Ellen lived in Kansas City before she came to Mercer.'

'Then we'll send a notice to the *Kansas City Star* newspaper,' the judge decided. 'Someone is bound to know something.'

Inside, Beth disagreed. If Ellen hadn't discussed her personal affairs with her closest friends she certainly wouldn't have discussed them with casual acquaintances.

The judge closed the file and rose. Beth bounded to her feet, as did everyone else. Wearing a huge smile, he thrust out his hand to her. 'Congratulations, Ms Trahern. You may take Daniel home.'

She pumped his arm, thrilled beyond words. 'Thank you, sir.'

Edith White snapped her briefcase closed. 'I'll be in touch.'

With a squirmy bundle in her arms, Karen Johnson approached. 'He's been such a good baby, I almost hate to give him up.' Her eyes glimmered with tears. 'I'm being silly. Regardless of how long they stay with us, I tend to get emotional when they leave.'

Having seen her treatment of Daniel firsthand, Beth sympathized.

Karen held the bundle out to Beth. 'I wish you two the very best.'

Beth settled Daniel in the crook of her arm and stared at his face. He looked at her and blinked, before sticking two fingers in his mouth. Peace flowed into her heart like thick, gooey honey.

She raised her head to speak to Tristan. 'Thanks for sharing this moment with me.'

His smile revealed even white teeth. 'My pleasure.'

Good-looking family. Relaxing in his study, Mitch's whispered words before he'd left the courtroom echoed in Tristan's mind. The phrase popped into his head without warning at the oddest moments. Mitch's refrain haunted him wherever he went—not even his office gave him sanctuary.

Nancy's comments joined in with more memories to torture him. *You're young enough to have another family.*

He picked up a rubber band from the small stash he'd collected from the daily newspapers and shot it across the room.

He liked kids, which was why he'd chosen pediatrics as his specialty. Having them run through his house, laughing and yelling, seemed so right. But now it was impossible.

He catapulted five more rubber bands, idly aiming at the contrasting row of bricks on his fireplace. Each bounced harmlessly off the mantel.

Determined, he tried once more. This time the band broke, flying off at a tangent.

For the past few years his hopes and dreams had been like that broken rubber band—shattered, without any possibility of restoration. To compensate he'd reserved a large portion of himself to avoid future heartbreak. Now he wasn't sure if what he had left to give would satisfy a woman, much less a family. And yet he wanted to try.

* * *

'How's the new mom?' Mary Peabody asked when Beth appeared on the ward for the first time in a week.

Beth smiled. 'Good. I never dreamed it would be so hard to take him to a sitter after only seven days. How do women cope after tending their babies for six or eight weeks?'

'It's tough to leave the little tykes,' Mary commiserated. 'It gets worse, too, as they grow older. When my youngest turned two she stood at the door and cried for me to stay. I was ready to quit my job.'

'At least the hospital day care center agreed to keep him,' Beth answered. 'I can run over there on my breaks.'

The telephone warbled. Mary answered, grabbing her ever-ready pen and pad. As she listened her cheerful expression disappeared. 'A six-year old girl, having an acute asthma attack, is on her way. Apparently she didn't respond to treatment in ER. I want you to special her.'

Beth hurried to prepare a private room. She hoped they'd be able to reverse the girl's condition before it became worse, requiring mechanical intervention like a ventilator.

Treatment protocols ran through her mind from her days in ER. Fast-acting drugs, perhaps an antibiotic, would be required. She ripped open a package of tubing and hooked the flexible hose onto the oxygen valve in the wall.

Jessica Thomas arrived, the muscles in her face and neck straining and her breath rattling in her chest. Mr and Mrs Thomas stood near the doorway as Beth and Tristan untangled the myriad tubes connecting the child to the life-saving treatment. Finally the tiny girl with flaxen hair was settled in bed, sitting against the pillows with an oxygen canula inserted into her nose.

'Give her another dose of epinephrine and an albuterol breathing treatment,' Tristan ordered. 'Start an aminophylline IV. Repeat her blood gases too.'

Beth hurried to obey.

'We'll monitor Jessica closely,' he told the parents, who appeared to have aged ten years from worry. 'I'd tell you to go home but I know you won't. Why don't you walk around the hospital for a while? Get some fresh air?'

'Go ahead, Harold,' his wife said. 'I'll stay here until you get back.'

'We'll take good care of her,' Beth promised. 'There's coffee down the hall and to your right.'

Tristan and Mr Thomas strode into the hallway while Beth threw the used syringes into the sharps collector.

'Jessie always has trouble when the weather changes,' Mrs Thomas said. 'Alternating days of warm and cold at this time of year are tough, but she's never been this bad before. I *hate* fall.' She blew her nose before she spoke again, her voice clogged with tears. 'Will she be OK?'

Beth had been asked that question often. Unfortunately she couldn't predict the outcome. 'We're doing everything we can,' she said.

For the next few hours Beth monitored Jessica and hoped that the drugs would soon do their job.

Someone from the lab called in the latest blood gas report and Beth scribbled it down. She handed Tristan the page. 'She's not getting better.'

He ran his hand over his shortly cropped hair. 'We may have to use a ventilator.' His pain was palpable, and Beth's heart ached for the Thomases and for Tristan.

Beth returned to Jessica's room. For the next hour she mentally willed the girl to respond.

Shortly before eleven, in the dark hours of night when hope sinks to its lowest, Jessica's breathing changed.

Beth sidestepped Mrs Thomas, asleep in the chair. The rise and fall of the girl's chest seemed less pronounced, her breathing less labored. She rushed to alert Tristan, finding him stretched out on the sofa in the nurses' lounge with his eyes closed.

She touched his arm. 'Tristan,' she whispered.

He jumped, planting his feet on the floor. 'Is she—?'

'It's working.'

Tristan raced ahead of her to the room. He listened carefully, his face impassive. Finally his face broke into a smile. 'You're right.'

Mrs Thomas snapped out of her doze. 'She's better?'

He nodded. 'The worst is over.'

The woman slumped, closing her eyes. 'Thank God,' she replied. 'I'm going to call Harold.'

Tristan hugged Beth. 'We did it.'

She smiled up at him. 'I know.'

Suddenly the relief became something more highly charged. His head lowered to hers and his lips brushed against her mouth in a demanding kiss, a kiss not of comfort but of passion. Stunned at first, she leaned against his chest—wanting to give as well as receive.

She lost all sense of time and place, ignoring the constant sound of oxygen flowing and the distant ding of someone's call bell.

In the next instant he broke the contact, looking as

dazed as she felt. 'Ummm. We'd better get another blood gas.'

Her lips ached from the pressure, but she forced a reply through them. 'Right away.'

She made the call to Respiratory Therapy, wondering if Tristan had somehow changed the rules and forgotten to tell her.

As if sensing Beth's unbalanced composure, Daniel fussed for several hours after they came home. By the time he settled down to sleep it was three a.m.

Beth dozed. Deep in her dream, she barely heard Daniel's alarm. In a flash the sound registered and she sprang out of bed, dragging the quilts along with her in her haste and stumbling over them at the door.

Daniel lay motionless. On previous occasions the noise had seemed to startle him to wakefulness and he'd begun breathing. Not this time.

Frantically Beth flipped him onto his back and rubbed his chest. He didn't respond so she ripped his sleeper open to begin CPR. 'Come on, Daniel,' she cried, tasting fear in her mouth. 'Don't give up now.'

In the next instant he resumed breathing.

Tears of joy streamed down her face. Beth cradled him in her arms and sat on the double bed, unable to leave him to return to her own room. After nearly losing Jessica—and now Daniel—she couldn't go to sleep.

She held him until pink fingers of daylight appeared in the sky. After rechecking the monitor, she carefully laid him in his crib and took the fastest shower on record.

Daniel seemed none the worse for wear but Beth

bundled him up for a visit to Tristan's office the minute it opened.

'What's wrong?' he asked.

'He quit breathing this morning.'

'Let's have a look.'

After being measured and weighed, Tristan examined Daniel thoroughly. 'He's gained weight, which is good. I'll increase his caffeine dosage—that should help.'

Beth heaved a sigh of relief.

Tristan studied her. 'You didn't sleep last night after you got off work, did you?'

'No.' He frowned and she hastened to add, 'I will, though. I promise.'

But over the next few days she discovered that it was easier said than done. She dozed during Daniel's naptime, finding the short periods of sleep unsatisfying—especially when the slightest noise interrupted those hours. Tiredness became her constant companion until she awakened one morning with a scratchy throat and a low-grade fever. By the time she was due to report to work her temperature had risen to an alarming level.

She called in sick. Next she phoned Katie. Knowing that the EMT was on vacation, she hoped that the girl could watch Daniel for a short time. But Katie didn't answer.

Finally she crawled into Ellen's bed to steal a few hours of rest while Daniel slept.

From a distance she heard a baby's cry, then a voice similar to Tristan's. In her lethargic state the ability to distinguish between fact and dream-filled fiction escaped her. She struggled to throw back the covers.

A firm hand stopped her. Something cool touched

her forehead and she sighed. It felt so good.

'Tell me where it hurts,' the voice commanded.

'Throat.'

The same hand slid under her shoulders and a glass touched her mouth. 'Drink.'

As she licked her lips she was lowered onto the bed. The water revived her enough so that she recognized her surroundings. She was in her bed but why was Tristan here? Blinking her eyes to clear the hazy film, she croaked, 'What are you—?'

'I'll explain later.'

Beth rolled onto her side to pull herself up. 'Must see. . .about. . . Daniel.'

'Daniel's fine. Go to sleep.'

Something cold rubbed her hip. She felt a prick, then a burning sensation followed. 'Ow,' she mumbled. Trying to brush away the offending pain, a vise attached itself to her wrist.

'Done,' the deep voice said, before the blankets sheltered her in a warm cocoon.

Her mystery visitor woke her several times to press a glass of cool liquid to her mouth. 'Swallow,' he urged.

Unable to argue, she did as she was told, before sinking back into sleep. Occasionally she heard a female voice but couldn't force herself to investigate.

By early evening some twenty-four hours later her chills and hot flashes had disappeared. Coherence returned, although her body ached as if she'd run a marathon.

Tristan walked into the room, carrying a mug of hot tea. 'How do you feel?'

'It *was* you.' Beth flung one arm over her eyes. 'I thought I'd been dreaming.'

'No. Lucky thing too. You were really out of it.'

She glanced at her bedside table. 'Oh, my gosh. Daniel!' She tried to swing her legs over the edge, but she didn't have the strength to untangle them from the sheets.

'Is fine. That boy eats all the time, doesn't he?'

'Every few hours.' Her eyes narrowed. 'How do you know how often he eats? I just fed him before I went to sleep.'

'That was yesterday.'

'What?'

'Why don't I start at the beginning?' Tristan said. One side of the bed dipped under his weight.

'Please do. How did you get in?'

'I heard you'd called in sick so after my evening rounds I decided to stop and see how you were doing. You didn't answer my knock so I tested the door and found it unlocked.

'Daniel was screaming his head off and you were out of your head with fever. I got him settled, gave you a shot—by the way, you have strep throat—and stayed to keep an eye on both of you.'

Beth rubbed her hip, remembering a sting. The spot was still sore. 'You stayed. . .all night?'

Tristan nodded, his eyes holding an unmistakable twinkle. 'Daniel agreed to be quiet if he could watch the late late show.'

'What?'

He grinned. 'He's a night owl, isn't he?'

'Takes after his mother.'

'I'll have to remember that. How about a shower?'

'Sounds great, but don't you have office hours?'

'Not today. It's Saturday, remember?' He helped her to her feet. 'Can you manage by yourself?'

Clutching her robe, Beth shuffled a few steps toward the bathroom. 'I think so.'

'If I hear a thump I'll come running,' he warned.

'I'll be fine.' After a long soak in a tub of hot water she felt more human. She tied her hair back, knotted the belt at her waist and went in search of Daniel.

In the hallway she sniffed the air. Had Tristan been cooking, too? She wondered what he'd found to prepare; her cupboards were on the lean side.

Beth found Daniel in his room, perched on Tristan's shoulder and wearing only a diaper. The quilt Ellen had embroidered lay in a heap at the foot of the crib.

Tristan rummaged in a drawer for a clean sleeper, talking to the little guy who stared at him with trust. Touched by the sight, she hesitated in the doorway.

Chattering the entire time, he wrestled with squirmy arms and legs until the child was clothed. 'OK, sprout. We'll get dressed and then we'll find something good to eat. Which do you prefer—a juicy steak or a bottle?'

Daniel hiccuped.

'Yup, that's what I figured,' Tristan drawled in a John Wayne parody. 'A T-bone for the big guy and a bottle for his buddy. Hold the glass.'

A huge grin spread across Beth's face at Tristan's nonsensical conversation. Was ever a man so kind, generous, thoughtful and. . .lovable?

It was true. She loved Tristan Lockwood.

She'd suspected from the very beginning that she'd be susceptible to his charm if he ever directed any of it her way. Now that he had, under the guise of developing a congenial work relationship, she had foolishly fallen in love with the man. He'd made it clear that he'd never love anyone again.

Tristan turned around with the small boy ensconced in the crook of his arm. 'Well, look who's up and around, Daniel. Want to see Mom?'

Certain that her eyes mirrored her personal discovery, Beth lowered her gaze to Daniel. Tristan must never find out how she felt. The knowledge would make him feel ill at ease, which would rub off on her. Ultimately their work would suffer and that had to be avoided at all costs.

She held out her arms, taking the bundle Tristan so carefully handed over. Her nerve endings quivered as his fingers brushed against the swell of her breast.

Gazing on Daniel's small features, her eyes burned. What would have happened if Tristan hadn't come? She shuddered to think.

'I'm so grateful—'

He interrupted. 'How about something to eat? Nancy brought chicken noodle soup.'

She *had* heard a woman's voice. Forcing levity into her voice, she replied, 'No steak?'

'Maybe next time.'

Tristan followed her into the kitchen. She took a seat at the table, accepting the bottle he had ready. Soon he placed a steaming bowl of soup in front of her.

For a few minutes Daniel's slurps filled the otherwise silent air. A sense of awkwardness came over Beth. This was too domestic a scene—too close to her fantasy—for comfort.

A chair scraped the floor. Tristan sat. 'I've been thinking,' he began.

His earlier jovial expression had disappeared. A more serious one, similar to that of a bearer of bad news, took its place.

She swallowed. 'Yes?'

'It's tough, taking care of a baby by yourself. It seems ridiculous because you don't have to.'

Beth narrowed her eyes. 'I won't give him up.'

'I'm not asking you to even consider it. I just wondered how you would have managed if I hadn't happened by?'

'I called Katie but she's out of town,' she defended. 'Besides, I'm better now. By tomorrow I'll be great.'

'But what about next time?' he asked quietly.

He'd voiced her own fears. She chewed on her bottom lip. 'We'll do the best we can.'

Tristan rested his elbows on the table. 'I want to help you. Not just when you're sick either. Daniel needs a male influence in his life.'

'What are you saying?'

'I want to be his father. I want the three of us to be a family.'

Startled, Beth jerked the nipple out of Daniel's mouth. He wrinkled his face and wailed in protest. 'Sorry,' she murmured, poking it back between his gums.

Daniel clamped down with ferocity, shimmering teardrops clinging to his eyelashes like perfect diamonds. With him content again, she stared at Tristan. 'A family. Like a husband, wife and child?'

He nodded, his dark-eyed gaze fixed on hers.

Excitement fluttered through her. His request seemed like a dream, coming so soon after she'd realized that she loved him. Yet her memories raised a caution flag. 'Why?'

'For Daniel's sake.'

'I see.' Her hopes were dashed. 'This is rather sudden. Wouldn't you agree?'

'We've known each other for over a year,' he pointed out.

'But most of that time we weren't on the best of terms.'

He flinched. 'Maybe not, but the last few weeks have been enlightening. From what I've seen, we'd be good together. Daniel would get the attention he needs. You and I would both have the family we've always wanted. We'd all benefit.'

But what about to love, honor, and cherish? Unable to pose the question, she asked another. 'What if you find someone else? Someone you'll love like you loved Elise?'

He shook his head. 'Won't happen.'

Remembering their passionate kiss in Jessica Thomas's room, she had to ask, 'What are you expecting out of this marriage?'

His gaze didn't waver. 'A marriage in every sense of the word. It shouldn't pose a problem, since we're attracted to each other—it's been obvious on several occasions.'

Beth felt her temperature rise, remembering those incidents with great detail.

'I won't rush you, though.' He drew a deep breath. 'I also expect honesty and fidelity.'

She cleared her throat. 'I want the same things,' she said, wishing that her voice didn't sound hoarse. If she'd had the courage she'd have added one more requirement—love. But, sadly, boldness had never been her strong suit so she reserved that point in her heart.

He paused. 'So, shall we get married?'

Beth stroked Daniel's downy head. She would do anything for Ellen's son, but marriage? To a man who didn't love her?

And yet she found the idea exciting. She could count the number of men she'd dated in her lifetime on one hand. Those relationships had never even remotely progressed to a wedding discussion.

Though she'd daydreamed of tying the knot with a handsome, successful prince-to-her-Cinderella, she'd never expected it to become a reality.

There's no such thing as a second chance. Ellen's timeless words of wisdom floated to the forefront of her memory.

Peace stole over her heart. She knew what she had to do. For Daniel, and for herself.

Taking a deep breath, she met his gaze. 'I'll marry you.'

CHAPTER NINE

TRISTAN blinked, as if he wasn't sure he'd heard correctly. In the next instant a slow, easy grin crossed his face. He leaned back in his chair, looking very comfortable and very pleased with himself. 'A sensible woman. I was prepared to counter every objection you might have.'

Annoyance budded. Somehow, she didn't think that Cinderella's prince had ever called *her* 'sensible'—and certainly not after his marriage proposal. Then again, the fairy-tale couple had married for love—not for a child's sake. Her irritation drained away as fast as it had materialized.

'Sounds like you've given this a lot of thought,' she said, keeping her tone light.

'Some,' he conceded.

'How will your family take the news? This is rather sudden.'

'They'll be thrilled. Especially after they meet you and Daniel.'

She wasn't convinced. 'What about your friends?' she asked, thinking of Mitch Adams and the others in his social circle. Maybe she should have asked these questions before she'd agreed to his proposal.

'My friends don't dictate my actions. Don't worry, they'll find you charming.' As if he understood her misgivings, he flashed one of his lopsided smiles. 'I won't make you plan a nine-course meal for fifty. At least not the first month we're married.'

She smiled at his gentle teasing.

'Seriously, my entertaining has been on a very small, low-key scale.'

Somewhat comforted by his reassurances, she nodded. 'How soon did you want to. . .um. . .want to. . .' The words stuck in her throat.

'Get married?' he asked. 'Right away.'

'Right away?' she echoed.

'There's no reason to delay, is there?'

'No, but. . .'

'We'll find a justice of the peace, or a minister if you prefer, set a date and we're in business.'

Her dreams of a long white gown, an organ bellowing out Wagner's 'Bridal Chorus', a church full of friends and an ornate six-layer cake vanished.

'How about a week from—?'

'Thanksgiving weekend. The end of November,' she stated. His inquisitive glance made her add, 'Naomi and Kirsten were coming to visit anyway. I want them to be there.' That was one point she would not negotiate.

Tristan stroked his chin. 'Less than a month away. That probably would work better. Give us time to make a few decisions, hire a housekeeper.'

'A housekeeper?'

He glanced around the room. 'I never noticed it before but your kitchen echoes.' His face turned serious. 'Yes, a housekeeper. If I get called to the hospital while you're working I can't bring Daniel along.'

She chewed on her lip. 'True.'

'I could drop him off at the employee childcare center,'

he mused, 'but in an emergency I won't have time. And what if he's sick or cranky?'

'It's fine, Tristan. So you won't mind if I keep my job?'

'No. But I do expect Daniel to come first.'

'He will,' she promised. 'Having the wedding near the end of the month will work out best anyway since I'm scheduled to leave Pediatrics by the first of December.'

He stared at her as if a wart had just sprouted on the end of her nose.

'My assignment was only temporary,' she hastened to add. 'Someone had to cover while one of the regular peds nurses took time off. I'm going back to ER.'

Unable to hold his gaze, she looked at Daniel. The wide-eyed attention he'd given his dinner began to ebb. His eyelids grew heavy, then bounced up as he fought against sleep. His mouth worked the nipple, then relaxed for a few seconds before he suckled again.

'Funny how you haven't been on the children's unit long, and yet it's hard for me to imagine you not being there.'

'Thanks for the vote of confidence.'

'Do you want Emergency Room duty again?' He spoke tentatively, as if afraid of her answer.

She smiled, recognizing his uncertainty. 'It isn't a question of what I want. I go where I'm assigned.'

He drew his eyebrows into a thick, dark line. 'I can talk to—'

Beth reached across the table for his hand. 'I don't want to capitalize on being your wife. I like Peds, and I like the ER. But if I had a choice I'm not sure which one I'd pick.' She chuckled. 'Ask me again after Dr

Sullivan retires. The new doctors may have me begging for a transfer.'

Daniel sighed a sweet baby sigh. His eyelids fluttered one final time before they closed, allowing his long lashes to rest on his cheeks. His jaw hung slackly and a few drops of formula trickled out of his mouth. Seeing Daniel so relaxed suddenly made her realize the extent of her own exhaustion.

'He's out for the count,' Tristan remarked, moving behind her. 'I'll put him to bed.'

His hand slid under Daniel's neck and shoulders, making contact with her breast. Startled by his touch, Beth drew a breath. At the same time she craved a more deliberate physical encounter.

For the next few seconds neither moved. Finally he spoke. 'Does it bother you? If I touch you, Bethany?'

Awareness flowed through her like a river of liquid heat. Her love welled up with an intensity that made her knees tremble. 'No,' she whispered, grateful that she had been sitting down.

'Good,' he responded. In the next instant he'd taken Daniel, leaving her arms empty and feeling strangely bereft. He disappeared in the direction of the nursery but Beth couldn't follow. She needed a few minutes to regain her composure—to settle her nerves.

A few minutes later he returned. 'You're next.'

'I'm not going to bed,' she protested. 'I'm not tired.' An urge to yawn came over her, but she clamped her jaws shut.

'OK. I won't argue.' He ushered her into the living room and pointed to the sofa. 'Maybe you'll feel like sleeping after you watch the news.'

She sat, surprised to see Tristan plop down beside her. At first she followed the CNN broadcast, but her eyelids grew heavy. Five minutes later she caught herself nodding off.

Tristan's large hand guided her head to his shoulder and he tucked her body under his arm. She snuggled close, resting her ear against his chest. Lulled by the steady beat of his heart and his fingers gently stroking her cheek, she drifted toward dreamland.

A piercing beep brought her upright. It only took a few seconds to identify the noise. 'Daniel,' she breathed.

Tristan's long strides carried him to the room before Beth had skirted the coffee-table. Daniel's cry stopped her in her tracks; relief made her sink onto the closest chair.

'He's fine,' Tristan said, rejoining her a few minutes later. 'The monitor came unplugged. He's asleep again.'

'I'd better stay in his room,' she decided, rising.

'No.'

His vehemence startled her and she jumped. 'No,' he repeated, this time in a more tempered tone. 'You'll go to your bed.'

'But what if I don't hear him?' she wailed.

'Then *I* will.' At her questioning glance, he added, 'I'm staying the night.'

Although she found the prospect of sharing Daniel's care until she regained her strength immensely comforting, she knew how devastating gossip could be. 'But what if someone tries to reach you?'

'It isn't unheard-of for a man to be found at his fiancée's apartment.' He tugged her through the doorway.

'Now go to bed,' he instructed, before leaving the room.

Beth untied her robe. She'd wait a few minutes until he'd settled in front of the television. Then she'd sneak into the nursery. Just as she'd decided that enough time had elapsed and that it was safe to institute her plan Tristan reappeared.

She jumped. 'You scared me.'

'Only because you aren't in bed,' he said, a cheeky grin on his face. He stripped off his knit polo shirt and unbuttoned the top button of his trousers.

'What are you doing?' Her exhaustion had vanished, leaving her wide awake.

'Making sure you stay in bed.' He crawled under the covers and held up the ones on her side so that she could slide under. 'Come here.'

She glanced away, ill at ease.

'Please,' he murmured in a whisper-soft voice, much like the one an adult used with a shy or reluctant child. Which was exactly how she felt.

The red mark extending down her neck and past her collar-bone suddenly seemed as noticeable as a flashing neon sign. Her low-cut nightgown revealed every inch of the port-wine stain she had managed to hide from everyone. She covered it with her left hand.

'Don't,' he admonished.

She rolled her fingers into a fist, keeping her hand at her throat. Inching her hand away, she finally dropped her arm to her side. With slow steps she approached the bed. Part of her wanted his touch, begged for the intimacies of marriage, yet she didn't know if she was emotionally ready. She loved him, yes, but she hadn't got used to the idea of him being her husband, much less her lover.

The gleam of satisfaction in his eyes comforted her. She might not be beautiful but he didn't find her repulsive.

She slid between the sheets, wishing that they were satin rather than cotton and smelled of rose petals rather than fabric softener. It was too bad that someone—anyone—hadn't ever mentioned the protocol for situations like this.

Once she'd stretched out she realized how the mattress sagged in the middle. With Tristan's weight on the other side, she rolled onto him. Trying to lever herself away, her hand clutched the juncture of his thighs.

He jumped. She stiffened.

'I'm not so sure this was a good idea,' he said, his voice oddly pitched. 'Are you willing to anticipate our wedding night?'

'Hmm. Well.' Coherent thought fled. At the same time the feel of his skin against hers sent a warm trickle down her spine.

'Have you ever—?'

Knowing what he was asking, she interrupted before he could finish. 'No.'

He grabbed her hand and gently brought it to rest on his waistline. 'I thought not,' he said.

Afraid to ask but wanting to know, she asked, 'Are you upset?'

'No, I'm not,' he answered. 'Get some rest, Bethany.'

She relaxed at the pleased note in his voice. Burrowing against his body, she breathed in his unique scent. Before sleep claimed her she realized something interesting. He always called her by her formal name, Bethany. Someday she'd ask him why.

Mercer Memorial Hospital's sign shone through the mid-November darkness like a lighthouse beacon.

'Nervous?' Tristan asked as he escorted Beth out of the cold and into the warm building via the doctors' entrance. He helped her shrug off her cozy but inelegant winter parka and hung it on a coat rack.

Beth smoothed the collar of her blue silk blouse. 'A little,' she admitted.

'Don't be,' he admonished. 'This is a perfect way to announce our engagement.' With his hand at the small of her back, he guided her through the hospital corridors to the conference room set aside for Amos Sullivan's retirement party. Beth noticed the enquiring glances sent in their direction, and understood why. Tristan presented a dashing figure in his dark suit and maroon shirt.

She smiled, reveling in the fact that soon her name, her future, would be linked to his. Life had definitely taken a turn for the better.

The sound of laughter and voices drifted through the hallways long before they reached their destination. Tristan's gentle pressure propelled her through the throng until they located the man of the hour.

Tristan extended one hand, keeping the other on Beth's waistline. 'Happy retirement, Amos.'

Beth echoed the sentiments.

'Thank you both,' Amos exclaimed, his pale eyes gleaming with obvious delight over his celebration.

'What are your plans?' Tristan asked.

'Betty and I will travel. I intend to do some locum

work once in awhile.' Amos winked. 'I'm glad to see you two are getting along so well.'

Conscious of his gaze following the path of Tristan's arm, Beth fought the blush trying to overtake her face.

Tristan leaned forward to make himself heard over the din. 'Beth and I are getting married.'

Amos chortled with glee. 'I had a feeling about you two. Congratulations.' He turned to Beth. 'Does this mean Mercer is losing a good nurse?'

Beth grinned. 'Afraid not. I'm coming back to ER. It won't be the same without you.'

'Maybe not, but change is sometimes for the better. My replacements are bright young men, full of new ideas. They'll be good for the hospital and the community.' He nodded in the direction of two men Beth had never seen before.

'Before you check into a nursing home remember that it took a pair to replace you,' Tristan said.

Amos laughed. 'You do know how to make an old man feel good. Come on. I'll introduce you to your new colleagues.' But before they could reach the two physicians someone stopped Tristan for a consultation. Amos propelled Beth forward.

She caught sight of a red-haired man of about medium height and a sandy-haired fellow who matched Tristan's size. Although both were nice-looking and probably in their early thirties, something in the taller one's hazel eyes drew her.

'Michael Knox and Jim Berkley,' Amos acknowledged. 'I'd like to introduce you to Beth Trahern. She's one of our best ER nurses.'

'All of Mercer's nurses are the best,' she corrected

with a smile, greeting each in turn. 'But I'm pleased to meet you. I understand that one of you will cover only a few days a week.'

'That's already changed,' the light-haired Berkley announced with a distinct Texas drawl. 'I'll be here full time as well, although my rotation will overlap with the weekend resident coverage.'

'That's wonderful. Our Friday and Saturday nights have always been hectic,' Beth said.

The hospital administrator garnered Amos while another physician steered Michael away, leaving Beth alone with Jim. Feeling it rude to desert this quiet man as well, she remained. 'Will your family be joining you?'

'I'm not married.' His gaze landed on her ringless finger. 'You?'

'Engaged,' she said proudly. 'We haven't had time to look for a ring yet.'

'Congratulations.'

His tone was polite, but Beth sensed an undercurrent of pain in his voice. Thinking that it was related to the trace of sadness in his eyes, she gambled at the reason. 'Didn't she want to move to Mercer?'

Jim blinked. 'How did you know?'

She raised one eyebrow. 'Woman's intuition.'

He twisted his mouth into a weak imitation of a smile. 'We broke up several months ago. We'd gotten along so well that it came as a complete surprise to me.' He sighed. 'I guess it's for the best.'

Beth laid a hand on his arm. 'I'm sorry.'

He shrugged. 'I don't know why I'm telling you this.'

'I don't mind listening.'

He studied her face. 'You seem familiar, for some reason.'

'Kindred spirits,' she quipped.

This time his smile was genuine. 'Must be. Too bad you're spoken for.'

A hand snaked around her waist. 'Sorry we got separated.'

Recognizing Tristan's familiar touch and scented after-shave, she turned toward him and beamed. 'I was beginning to wonder if you'd got lost.'

'Not a chance,' Tristan declared. He extended his right hand, which the other physician accepted. 'Tristan Lockwood.'

'James Berkley.'

'Tristan is my fiancé,' Beth interrupted. 'He's one of our pediatricians.' She couldn't help but compare the two men. Although Berkley was personable, he simply didn't make her heart pound like Tristan did.

'You're a lucky man,' Jim replied.

'I know.' The chief of staff arrived with several others in tow. 'We won't monopolize your time,' Tristan remarked. 'Nice meeting you, Jim.'

'I'll look forward to working with you, Beth,' Jim said.

'Same here.'

As soon as Tristan had steered her out of the crowd pressing in on them Beth commented, 'He seems like a decent guy.'

'Yes, well, we'll see what kind of physician he is. Are you ready to go?'

Startled by his curtness and the abrupt change of subject, Beth stared at him in amazement. 'I thought you wanted to stay until Dr Sullivan received his gift?'

His clipped tone softened. 'You're right. It's still early.'

For the next hour Beth fielded a multitude of congratulations, pleased at how everyone seemed genuinely happy for Tristan. Tristan never left her side, as if he sensed that she didn't want to cope with the well-wishers alone.

For a while she fell into her role of an excited fiancée. But her brightness dimmed the moment she allowed herself to remember the reason for their marriage. Tristan hadn't chosen her for herself—he'd chosen her so that he could have a son.

Naomi telephoned early the next morning. 'I'm telling you, Beth, Ellen's mystery man never worked in Chicago. Kirsten and I have checked with each hospital for men with those initials who also have some type of medical background. We haven't come up with a single promising lead. I'm beginning to wonder if he even exists.'

'He has to,' Beth replied dryly. 'We didn't find Daniel under a cabbage leaf.'

'Maybe Daniel's daddy was only there for a few days, like Ellie was. If so we'll never find him, even if we hired professional help.' She paused. 'You weren't thinking of contacting a private investigator, were you?'

'No. I don't have the money and I can't very well ask Tristan for it. Besides, the court will try to find him.'

'Rest easy. I doubt the man will ever show up to challenge you for custody.'

'I hope you're right.'

'In a few months Tristan will be Daniel's father in every sense of the word,' Naomi replied. 'And, although you can tell him about Ellen, *you* will be his mother.'

'You're right. You will come to the wedding, won't you? It will be a quiet affair in the hospital chapel.'

'We wouldn't miss it. Kirsten's already making a list of things we need to bring for our long weekend. See you then.'

Beth replaced the receiver. Naomi's lack of success had given Beth a clear conscience about the three of them becoming a family. She'd worried over what she'd do if they discovered Daniel's biological father, but now she could put those fears to rest.

Thrilled over the positive changes in her life, she hummed a few bars of a children's song, 'If You're Happy and You Know It'. She couldn't ever recall feeling so excited or enthusiastic about her future.

'Come on, Danny boy,' she called out. 'Time to leave for the hospital.'

Before the clock's hands reached two she and Daniel were on their way out the door. By two-thirty she was on the peds unit, ready for report. 'You should have a quiet evening,' one of the day nurses commented. 'Most of the cases are straightforward; no one is critically ill. Paula Rossiter could give you some trouble, though. She's scheduled for a spinal fusion tomorrow and she's tense.'

'Has anyone explained the procedure to her?' Beth asked.

'The orthopedic surgeon,' the nurse answered. 'I've asked if she has any questions but she claims she doesn't. Says she's heard all she wants to hear.'

'I'm sure her lengthy recovery period weighs on her mind,' Beth mused. 'Being immobilized in a cast for four to five weeks is tough for anyone, much less an active teenager.'

'Yeah, well, good luck. I have a feeling she'll run you ragged tonight.'

Beth nodded. She'd make a point to spend extra time with the fifteen-year-old girl and spread some of her happiness around.

But as the evening wore on Beth was grateful that the rest of the unit was quiet. Paula's call bell rang constantly and her demands didn't end.

'Can't I have a milkshake?' the girl whined.

'You had one earlier,' Beth replied firmly. 'You're officially NPO, which means you can't eat anything else this evening. I'm sorry.'

The brunette's sullen expression grew to a pout. Angrily she clicked the television on, turning up the volume to blaring levels.

Beth confiscated the remote control. 'Look,' she began, 'I know you're worried about the surgery, but being a brat won't change things. You might try a positive attitude—it usually works wonders.'

'I'll be stuck here for weeks. My friends will forget me while I'm in this lousy hospital,' Paula wailed.

Suddenly Beth understood. She sat on the edge of the bed. 'True friends won't forget you or let you suffer by yourself. Once they know they can visit any day of the week and telephone almost any time you'll have such a steady stream of classmates that we'll have to appoint a social secretary.'

Wiping her tear-filled eyes, Paula giggled. 'I guess.'

The door opened and a girl peeked her head inside. 'Hi, Paula. Can we come in?'

Beth patted Paula's hand. 'What did I tell you?' she whispered. She left the room with the sound of girlish chatter ringing in her ears.

She'd barely entered the nurses' station when the telephone jingled. 'Peds, Beth speaking,' she answered crisply.

'It's Katie. Remember that Weller kid who swallowed the bottle of acetaminophen some time ago?'

'Yes.'

'He's on his way up.'

'More pills?'

'Nope. He swallowed a penny this time. It's lodged sideways in his esophagus.'

'Good heavens.'

'No kidding. That boy needs constant supervision.'

'I'll make sure everything is tied down in his room,' Beth promised.

'Good. By the way, tonight is Dr Berkley's first night on duty. He's quite a guy.'

Beth smiled. The young physician with sad eyes had obviously activated Katie's mothering instincts.

'Got to go. Have fun.'

The elevator doors whooshed open and the Wellers stepped out. The parents looked tired, wearing what-will-he-do-next expressions on their faces. The aide accompanying them handed Beth the child's chart before she left.

'Let's get you settled,' she told the small family.

'I know it looks as if I don't watch him,' Mrs Weller said, sounding defensive, 'but I do.'

'Children are very inquisitive at this age,' Beth

answered. 'Exploring with their mouths is part of their learning process.'

'I sweep our floors morning, noon and night. Where he found that penny I'll never know.'

'Do you have a play-pen for him?'

'No. But we're going to get one,' his mother declared. 'Maybe it will keep him out of trouble.'

Beth flipped open the folder to read the physician's orders. Toby was scheduled for an endoscopy first thing in the morning, which meant that she had the usual pre-surgical tasks to perform.

She started to close the folder but something stopped her. Wondering if she'd missed an important instruction, she reread the hand-written orders and scanned the physician's signature. Dr J.D. Berkley. No, she hadn't overlooked a thing.

She closed the chart. This time, however, something in her subconscious clicked. A surge of adrenalin made her heart pound. Frantic, she rifled through the pages to find the document she'd seen earlier.

This time she ignored the content of the orders and studied the writing itself. It looked familiar. Too familiar. She scrutinized the signature. His middle initial had escaped her notice before, but now it stood out. Berkley.

Her heart leaped into her throat. Jim Berkley couldn't be Daniel's father. Could he?

CHAPTER TEN

BETH performed her duties by rote. Thoughts of Daniel ranked uppermost in her mind. What would she do—how would she survive—if she lost him?

Jim Berkley couldn't be his father. She struggled to remember every word of her conversation with Dr Berkley, hunting for clues to either prove or disprove his parentage of Daniel. Nothing came to mind; he hadn't said anything the night of the party to indicate that he had any ties to Ellen. Beth was simply overreacting.

No matter how often she declared to herself that it was only a coincidence she couldn't dispel her doubts. Vowing to learn the truth, she went to ER during her supper break and found the young physician enjoying a mug of coffee in the nurses' station.

His face brightened when he saw her. 'Get the Weller boy settled in?'

Hiding her fear behind a smile, she nodded as she poured coffee into a Styrofoam cup. 'He's lucky he didn't choke to death. Someone told me that's how Lifesavers candy came about. Apparently the inventor was either afraid that a child could choke or knew someone who had so he designed his treat in the shape of a disc with a hole in the middle. Fascinating story.'

'Kids will swallow anything. I've had them come in with everything from watch batteries to bed springs. I'll never forget a case I had in Chicago. The mother was getting ready for a party and her daughter swallowed a diamond earring. What a night! The mom acted more concerned over her jewelry than her child. She waited outside the OR for it, too.' He shook his head, his eyes twinkling at the memory.

Beth picked up on one word. 'You're from Chicago?'

'No, Dallas. I was in the Windy City almost a year ago. A friend of mine went on his honeymoon so I covered his practice for about ten days.'

The time frame matched. 'Is your ex-girlfriend from Texas too?'

'Kansas City. I met her in Chicago, though. She was there for a medical records meeting and developed bronchitis. Someone brought her to the office and I wrote her a prescription. I ran into her later—we both stayed in the same hotel—had a few drinks, exchanged addresses.' He drained his coffee-mug and set it on the desk.

Beth's doubts now grew into certainties. She wanted to run from the room and pretend that she'd never heard of Jim Berkley, but her feet refused to move.

'Things clicked between us. We met a few times in Oklahoma City as it was halfway between us. She even met my family so she knew I was serious about her. Then, out of the blue, she wrote and said it was over. I tried to find her but she'd quit her job and moved. Her boss said she went to St Louis. The private detective never found her.'

'Are you still searching?'

'Not actively. Until I get another lead I'm biding my time.'

'Why do you think she left?'

He threw up his hands. 'Meeting my family spooked

her. Somehow she had the idea that with her background she didn't fit into the Berkley line. It never mattered to me that she couldn't trace her ancestry back three hundred years.'

His explanation made sense. Ellen had never had a surplus of self-esteem.

A nurse who Beth occasionally worked with approached. 'Dr Berkley? We're ready for you in Room One.'

'Be right there.' He rose. 'I always seem to unload my problems on you.'

'That's OK.' Beth's smile was weak. 'See you around, Jim.'

He skirted the counter then turned back. 'By the way, my friends call me J.D.'

She froze. 'Oh?'

He grinned. 'It's short for James Daniel.'

The blood drained from her face, sending a chill through her body as effectively as if the room temperature had dropped thirty degrees. 'Sure.'

Beth made her way back to Pediatrics, aware of only one thing. Fate had brought Daniel's father to Mercer, causing her hopes and dreams—her future—to collapse. Not only would she lose Daniel but she would lose Tristan as well. He'd said that he wouldn't love anyone again, making it clear—at least in her mind—that their upcoming marriage was because of Daniel.

Hollow-eyed, she finished her shift, pretending that her life was story-book perfect. On the surface it was like a dream come true, she had a beautiful baby boy and a handsome, successful physician-fiancé. Underneath, her stomach churned with frustration and gut-wrenching disappointment. Her sole wish was to go home and lick her wounds.

That night, as she tucked Daniel into his crib and covered him with the quilt Ellen had painstakingly created, she couldn't hold the tears back any longer.

Why did he have to come to Mercer! she railed silently at the walls. Of all places in Missouri, of all towns in the USA, why did he choose this one?

The hours wore on. While contemplating her options, she dusted every room except Daniel's, and scrubbed the kitchen until it was as sterile as a surgical suite.

She came to a few conclusions. Mercer was too small a community for secrets to be kept. Everyone knew of Ellen McGraw and how Beth had assumed responsibility for her son. Jim only had to mention Ellen's name and the missing pieces would fall into place. The only question was—did she want to supply them herself or let the man stumble across them on his own?

She rejected the latter thought, knowing that she only had one sensible option. She had to tell Dr Berkley—and Tristan—the truth. The question was when and how?

A short time later Beth jerked the front door open to admit Tristan. 'Thanks for coming so quickly.'

'What's going on?' he asked. 'What's wrong?'

She avoided his gaze. 'Have a seat. I have something to tell you.'

He perched on the edge of the sofa, his brow wrinkled with puzzlement.

'Do you remember the judge mentioning that the court would try to find Daniel's father?'

'Yes.' His face cleared. 'They found him?'

'The court didn't. I did.'

'You?'

'Actually, I stumbled across him. He's recently moved to Mercer. It's Dr Berkley.'

Tristan sank against the cushions, looking as if he'd been poleaxed. 'Jim Berkley? How?'

Beth summarized the story.

'Does he want Daniel?'

'I assume so. I haven't told him yet. I had to talk this over with you first.'

He ran his hands over his head. 'I don't know what to say.'

'I know.' She watched his reaction carefully.

Tristan shook his head. 'I seem to have rotten luck when it comes to families.'

She struggled to swallow the lump in her throat. Her luck didn't seem to be any better.

'This changes everything.'

'I know,' she repeated. Even though the room was cozy and warm, a bone-chilling cold had penetrated.

The silence in the quiet room grew deafening. 'When did you realize. . .?'

'Last night.'

'I'd like to be here when you tell him.'

'He should arrive any time.' She rubbed her arms. 'Maybe he won't want Daniel.'

Tristan stared at her. 'He'll want him,' he said grimly. 'If he were my son, I wouldn't give him up.'

Jim stared at the photo Beth handed to him—a color snapshot of Ellen. 'She's dead?' he asked, sounding shell-shocked.

'I'm sorry,' Beth murmured. She explained everything, ending with how she had realized that Jim was the J.D. of Ellen's letters.

Grief and resignation etched Jim's features. If she'd had any doubts about his feelings for her friend, they no longer existed. The poor man was devastated by the news.

She glanced over his bent head at Tristan. He nodded ever so slightly. Mustering a calm she didn't feel, she continued.

'Ellen left something precious behind.' She grabbed Jim's wrist. 'She had a son. Your son.'

Jim lifted his head. His eyes were suspiciously moist. 'She was pregnant?' he asked in a hoarse voice.

Beth nodded. 'The baby came early. He had a few problems but Tristan took marvelous care of him. Daniel is fine.'

'Daniel?'

She smiled. 'Ellen insisted on calling him Daniel James. I never knew why until you told me your full name. It seemed appropriate, though. He may not have had to face actual lions but he's encountered some frightening obstacles during his short life.'

'I have a son.' Wonderment filled Jim's voice. 'Where is he?'

'First door on your left.'

Tristan's beeper went off and he muttered under his breath. 'I hate to, but I've got to go,' he said, standing next to Beth. 'Will you be all right?'

'I'm OK. Besides, I have to be at work soon.'

'Then I'll see you later,' he promised.

After she'd closed the door behind him she went to the nursery and paused in the doorway. Jim, or J.D. as he preferred to be called, gazed down on the little baby with such love that her heart ached. At least she could console herself that Daniel wouldn't be neglected.

'He's beautiful, isn't he?' she remarked in a low tone.

J.D. gave Daniel a little pat on his raised rump and followed her from the room. 'You've taken good care of him. I appreciate that. I hope I can do as good a job.'

The prospect that he might choose to leave Daniel with her and Tristan faded. 'Then you'll be taking him?'

'Yes. You surely didn't think I'd—?'

Beth shrugged. 'I didn't know what to think. Especially since Ellen was adamant that I keep the baby.'

'I appreciate your and Tristan's gesture. But Daniel is my son and I want him. He's all that I have left of Ellen.'

'I understand.' In the morning's wee hours she'd debated fighting for Daniel but knew she wouldn't win. She'd fought enough battles to learn which ones would be lost. This was one of them.

'You'll have other children.'

How could she say that her marriage centered around Daniel? That the reason for a wedding—to care for the boy—no longer existed? 'Probably.'

His eyes narrowed. 'You can't have children?'

'It isn't that.' She paused, wondering how much to divulge. Then she decided to be honest. 'Tristan and I agreed to marry because of Daniel. We both wanted a family—he lost his, you see. Anyway, this seemed the best way for each of us to get what we wanted.'

'You don't love each other?' he asked, incredulous.

She pulled at a loose thread on the hem of her sweater. 'Daniel was his—our—prime concern.'

A furrow appeared in his forehead and his eyes narrowed. 'Tristan gave me a distinct "hands-off" impression at the party. Are you sure you understand his motives?'

'I'm positive.' Finding the subject too painful, she changed it. 'I'll contact my lawyer and see what needs to be done to sort out the legal tangles.'

'I'll have to find other living quarters,' Jim said. 'Do you mind if Daniel stays here until then?'

'No problem. You can take all of his things. They aren't fancy but Ellen picked them out.'

He fell silent. 'If you and Tristan go your separate ways maybe you'd consider moving in with me.'

Beth snapped to attention. 'What?'

'To look after Daniel. Be his nanny or whatever you want to call it. If you wanted to, *we* can get married.' He pressed on. 'You'd fulfill your promise to Ellen.'

How unbelievable to receive two proposals within a few weeks. The idea was tempting. Too tempting. Yet she didn't have trouble making a decision. She couldn't ignore the truth—she'd accepted Tristan's proposal because she loved him. Providing for Daniel was important, but she knew that she could have done so without Tristan's help. J.D. was a nice man but he wasn't Tristan.

'I'll help you and Daniel in any way I can.' Beth smiled to soften her next words. 'But I can't live with you in any capacity.'

He stepped closer until their bodies nearly touched. 'Are you sure?' His head lowered, making his intentions plain. His hands clasped her shoulders and he paused, as if waiting for an objection.

She gave none. J.D.'s mouth brushed against her cheek in a gentle peck before his rock-hard lips zeroed in on hers. She breathed in his musky scent and tried to return his kiss.

Even though she willed it, the brief intimacy didn't stir her inner being like Tristan could. It was similar to kissing a family friend, or even a brother—nice, but lacking the ardor she wanted and expected.

He stepped back, dropping his hands to his sides.

'I'm sorry,' she said, silently begging Ellen's forgiveness. 'I'd rather be your friend.'

'I had a feeling you'd say that. If you should change your mind. . .' His boyish face held hope.

Slowly she shook her head. 'I won't.' Having once had a taste of passion, she couldn't settle for anything less.

Once again Beth sat in Judge Winters's courtroom. She hardly listened to the proceedings, knowing only that at the sound of his gavel Daniel would cease to be her responsibility. Her stint as a mother had lasted exactly one month.

Her promise to Ellen had echoed through her mind again, just as it had ever since J.D. had suggested their own marriage of convenience. She had failed her best friend.

Maybe she should accept. She and J.D. got along well enough. Wasn't companionship just as important as romance?

A loud thump brought her out of her reverie. Her guardianship had been rescinded. Daniel was now officially remanded into his father's custody.

Beth reached inside the carrier and gathered Daniel close to her heart. She squeezed him tight and blinked back the tears forming behind her eyelids. He squealed in protest and she smiled. 'Here's your daddy, Daniel. Be happy for Aunt Beth. OK?' She pressed a kiss to his downy head and breathed in his baby scent. In the future she'd hold him, feed him, diaper him, but never again would she perform those loving tasks as his mother.

Pain shot through her chest. She handed him over to J.D., unable to stop the tear trailing down her cheek.

'You'll still be a big part of his life, Beth,' J.D. said softly. 'You were Ellen's best friend. You'll be another link to his mother.'

She wiped away the moisture collecting on her face. Her lower lip quivered. 'I appreciate the thought.' Clearing her throat, she added, 'You can come for the rest of his things any time.' With that, she hurried from the courtroom.

Rounding the corner, she ran into Tristan. He caught her before she stumbled down the stairs. 'I tried to get here sooner,' he began, 'but I ran into a few problems with a patient.'

Touched by his consideration, the lump in her throat threatened to rise. 'Thanks, but it's over.'

His grip on her shoulders didn't lessen. 'How are you doing?'

She shrugged, unable to voice her thoughts.

'It's like having a death in the family, isn't it?' he asked, the expression in his eyes tender.

She nodded, surprised by his astuteness. 'How did you know?'

'Daniel was mine, too.'

'Yes, well, now he's J.D.'s. Our lives can get back to normal.'

'What do you mean?'

She squared her shoulders and swallowed. 'There's no need to get married. Our reason no longer exists.'

He fell silent. 'We don't need to make a decision today.'

'Why postpone the inevitable?'

'Are you sure this is what you want?'

No, she screamed inside. I want you to love me. I want us to start a family of our own. 'It's for the best.' Her composure began to slip. 'Got to go, Tristan. I'll be late for work.'

She broke out of his hold. Through a haze of tears she tripped down the stairs, determined to find a private place before she broke down. Ignoring the staccato sound of her heels on the marble and the echo in the quiet halls, she raced to her car. Now came the impossible task of picking up the pieces.

Anxious to be among friends, Beth drove the three hours to Kansas City after her shift ended on Wednesday night. She couldn't bear to be in her house over the Thanksgiving holiday, especially after her wonderful plans had soured.

Once again doubts assailed her. 'I shouldn't have told J.D. the truth,' she confided to Naomi and Kirsten. 'Maybe he would have never found out about Ellen.'

Naomi slung an arm around Beth's shoulder. 'Let's be realistic. You might have gotten away with it in Kansas City, but in a town the size of Mercer?' She shook her head. 'Not only that, but a lot of people either knew Ellen or heard about her after the accident. Somewhere along the line word would have leaked out.'

Naomi softened her tone. 'I know you. You wouldn't

have been able to live with the secret. Every morning you'd have wondered if that was the day J.D. would learn the truth. Once he had he might not have been so understanding, either.'

Beth winced at her last statement. At least he hadn't forbidden Ellen's friends from seeing Daniel. She didn't know how she'd cope if he had.

'I had a twelve-year-old boy the other day who came into ER in a diabetic coma,' Kirsten began. 'He'd realized that his mother had kept him from his father all those years, claiming he'd died when they'd only divorced. To punish her he skipped his morning insulin and ate several candy bars for good measure. We pulled him through, but he has a lot more to deal with than just his medical condition. You don't want Daniel to grow up resenting you.'

'I know I did the right thing. But it's still hard,' Beth confessed. 'I just feel like I let Ellen down.'

'You did what you could. Ellen couldn't expect more than that.'

Beth nodded, pinching the bridge of her nose.

Naomi rose. 'Rest up. By the time you go home you'll have your life back on track.'

Somehow it didn't seem likely.

Leaning back in his chair, Tristan pulled a rubber band out of his lab coat pocket and aimed at the pencil standing upright in the cup on his desk. He let fly, certain that he'd hit the easy target. It shot wide of the mark and he grumbled his frustration. Yet he wasn't surprised—his whole Thanksgiving weekend had been a frustrating experience.

The wedding plans had dissolved for lack of a bride. In fact, he hadn't suffered through such a bleak holiday since the first one after Elise had died. He'd counted the hours until the four days had ended, looking forward to Monday and a busy office schedule. Now here he sat, waiting for his first patients to arrive.

He yanked open the top drawer and rummaged for another band. Finding several of the size he favored, he closed one eye and pointedly took aim.

The door creaked. Maeve, his nurse, poked her head inside. 'There's a Dr Naomi Stewart on line one. Are you available, Dr Lockwood, or would you rather return her call?'

'I'll take it now, Maeve,' he told her, wondering what Beth's friend wanted as he let his missile fly. Missed again. Shifting positions in his executive chair, he punched the lighted button. 'Lockwood.'

'I stumbled across some lab results this morning. I thought you should be aware of them,' Naomi said without preamble. 'Especially since they concern Daniel.'

His interest perked. 'What did you find?'

'Apparently Ellen had an alpha-fetoprotein blood test early in her pregnancy. The level was abnormally low. Her obstetrician had it repeated, and received the same results. She refused an amniocentesis.'

'Interesting,' he mused aloud. Obstetricians included the test in their pre-natal work-ups because it was a good screening tool. Elevated results indicated problems like spina bifida, while those at the opposite end suggested Down's syndrome. But, like many other tests, this wasn't an infallible procedure. Any woman with an abnormal result underwent amniocentesis for a more definitive diagnosis. Daniel's normalcy made it obvious that Ellen had had the dubious honor of being one of those with a false positive.

'I thought you should know. If you'd like I'll have copies of the medical record sent.'

'Appreciate it,' he said. 'By the way, have you heard that Daniel's father has been found?'

'Beth visited this weekend and told us all about it. We tried to understand Ellen's motives, but couldn't come up with much. Although, after obtaining this information, it's beginning to make sense.'

'Oh?'

'With the possibility of an abnormal child, and considering his background, Ellen expected J.D. to reject her. She made sure he couldn't by rejecting him first. It's so sad. Things could have turned out so differently for them.'

'How true.' He paused. 'How's Beth? I'd been trying to reach her, but. . .' His voice trailed away. If he couldn't talk to her while she worked on his unit, his chances of having an in-depth conversation when she transferred back to ER were nil.

'She's emotionally drained, but that's to be expected.' A pause filled the airwaves. Finally Naomi spoke. 'I've seen Beth and Ellen handle a variety of situations. They tended to react in a similar manner. I may be sticking my nose where it doesn't belong, but do you understand what I'm getting at?'

The pieces fell together as he recalled incidents in her home when she'd apologized before he could find fault. 'I think so. She broke our engagement so I couldn't.'

'I suspect so. The question is, and you don't have to

give me your answer, do you want it fixed?'

His spirits rose. 'Thanks for the tip,' he said, ending the conversation. But before he could make any plans Maeve poked her head inside his office once again.

'Dr Berkley would like a few minutes, if you're free.'

'Send him in.'

A few seconds later J.D. sank into the chair Tristan offered. 'I wanted to tell you how much I appreciate everything you've done for Daniel. Beth told me what lengths you were willing to go to for my son.'

'You have my sympathy over losing Ellen. Daniel won't take her place, but he'll help.'

'He already has, in ways you can't imagine. Then again, I suppose you can.' J.D. cleared his throat. 'I'm here because I wondered if you wanted to continue as Daniel's physician. If you'd rather not, I understand.'

Tristan picked up a rubber band and began stretching it. 'I'd be happy to, but it's more a case of what *you* want.'

J.D. grinned. 'I'd like you to be his pediatrician. No hard feelings?'

'No. Daniel's needs come first.'

J.D.'s smile faded. 'Beth said you felt that way.'

'She did?'

Daniel's father nodded. 'After she told me that things weren't working out between you two I asked her to move in with us.'

Rage welled up inside Tristan. Who did Berkley think he was? Beth had agreed to marry *him*. Then he remembered the scene on the courthouse steps—how she'd broken their engagement with a few terse words.

Fear gripped him. Had Beth's sense of honor to Ellen

been stronger than her promise to him? He forced himself to remain calm. 'Did she agree?'

'She's thinking about it.' J.D. clapped his hands on his thighs and rose. 'You have a full waiting room so I won't keep you. See you around.'

'Sure.' Alone again, he pictured his solitary future. Now that Daniel and Beth, especially Beth, weren't part of his life it stretched ahead bleak and lifeless. He clenched his fists until his hands ached. He refused to return to those dark days. He wouldn't.

Making a decision, he jumped to his feet in search of Maeve. 'Who's first?' he demanded.

A startled Maeve pointed to a room and handed him a chart. Tristan scanned the recorded symptoms. The sooner he finished here the sooner he could see Beth. If she chose Berkley over him so be it, but he wouldn't give in without a fight.

An outbreak of respiratory ailments and influenza kept Beth too busy to dwell on her personal life. With the steady influx of cases she barely had time to breathe, much less think about what might have been. Because of the extra demand on Pediatrics, her transfer to ER had been temporarily postponed.

'I've been trying to see you for the past three days. We need to talk, Beth,' Tristan said as she prepared a bed for another hospital admission.

'Is it about the Stephens boy's insulin?' she asked, being deliberately obtuse. 'I processed your new orders a few minutes ago.'

'Not about work. About us.'

'There isn't an "us". Besides, I can't right now, Tristan.

You've just admitted another case of viral pneumonia.'

'You're working too hard. I know you're pulling double shifts since you returned from the holiday.'

'A lot of nurses are,' she commented, dragging the plastic tent over the top of the crib. 'The bug going around is hitting the staff just as hard as the patients. Every able-bodied person has volunteered for extra duty.'

'It hasn't been that long ago since you were sick yourself. You have to take it easy. You don't need a relapse.'

'I'm fine. Really.'

'I see those circles under your eyes. Promise me you won't work another shift after yours ends at eleven.'

His concern was bittersweet. 'I promise. Besides, I'm working my second one now. We're not allowed to cover twenty-four hours.'

'Thank God,' he murmured. She brushed past him but he forestalled her by gripping her wrist. 'Don't make any decisions about Berkley until you hear what I have to say. OK?'

Puzzled by his vehemence and his statement, she nodded. Before she could dwell on his mysterious order her one-year-old patient had arrived.

She spent the next few hours dispensing medication, checking IVs and assisting the respiratory therapy technicians with breathing treatments for their small charges. At long last reinforcements arrived and Beth was free to leave.

Standing in the glow of the lamps lighting the hospital entrance, Beth turned up the collar of her well-worn nylon parka against the wind. She breathed in the night air, invigorated by its bite after long hours in the filtered atmosphere.

A figure detached itself from the shadows. She felt no fear, recognizing the familiar build before she saw his face. To be honest, she'd expected this confrontation—although she'd hoped it would wait until she wasn't both mentally and physically exhausted.

His comment caught her off guard. 'I love you, Beth.'

CHAPTER ELEVEN

BETH had never expected to hear those words from Tristan's mouth. Stunned, her jaw dropped.

Tristan moved out of the darkness and into the light. Standing an arm's length away, she saw his rosy cheeks and reddened nose, courtesy of the brisk air. A twinge of discomfort pierced her heart. She'd taken her time leaving the unit, hoping that if he had been waiting for her he'd have tired, given up and gone home.

'I know you love Daniel,' Tristan said, 'and I know you want to keep your promise to Ellen. But, please, don't move in with Berkley.' His voice held a note of desperation.

'How did you know he'd asked?'

'He told me. I also had a long discussion with Naomi.'

'You did? Why?'

'We—actually, it was Naomi—figured out why Ellen ran away from J.D. She'd had an abnormal alpha-fetoprotein test which, as it turned out, was false. Anticipating J.D.'s rejection, she rejected him first.' He took another step forward, his hands deep in the pockets of his overcoat. 'That's why you said we didn't need to get married. You were rejecting me so I couldn't reject you first.'

She studied a crack in the sidewalk. 'You said it was for Daniel's sake. You told me you could never love another woman like you loved Elise. Daniel was the glue holding us together. Without him we didn't have a chance.'

'Did you—*do* you—want a chance?'

'More than ever. But after I told you about J.D. you said that it changed everything.'

Tristan stared into the darkness. 'It did, but not like you thought. I'd planned to have my beautiful little family and keep part of myself closed off. But when my little dream bubble burst everything changed. I had to take a hard look at my motives.

'You see, I met Elise in college and we had instant fireworks. We had a wonderful life, and I wanted it recreated—to start where I'd left off. This time, however, I'd make sure I couldn't suffer the pain of loss.

'You stole into my heart until the embers I tried to extinguish finally became flames. Steady, unwavering flames. I tried to deny my feelings by claiming I only wanted to provide for Daniel. The truth is that I wanted you just as much.'

Beth sank onto the cement bench. 'Are you positive?'

He crouched down in front of her. Taking her cold hands in his warm ones, he said, 'Very much so. After the scene in the courthouse I planned to be noble and let you go, as long as you were happy. But when Berkley came into the picture I discovered that I couldn't give you up so easily. To be honest, I was jealous of him at Amos's retirement party.'

'You were?'

'Absolutely. I especially didn't like the idea of you going back to ER. I knew I wouldn't have a chance once you left Peds and were around him every day.'

'Were you responsible for the delay in my transfer?' she asked, narrowing her eyes.

'In a way. I asked the nursing supervisor if she'd consider keeping you on the children's unit until the crisis passed. She agreed.'

'I can't believe it.' A question she'd had for some time came to the fore. 'Why did you always call me Bethany? Never Beth.'

'Because I wanted to keep my distance. I suspected that if I ever relaxed my guard I'd fall in love. And I did.'

Tears of happiness streamed down her face. Tristan wiped them away with his thumbs. 'Oh, Tristan,' she wailed. 'The only reason I accepted your proposal was because I loved you too. I could have supported Daniel on my own but I didn't want to. I wanted *you* with us.'

He smiled. 'Does this mean that you and Berkley won't be—?'

'I refused the very first time he mentioned it,' she interrupted, stroking the side of his face. 'I couldn't imagine living with him when you were the first one I wanted to see every morning and the last one to see at night. I suffered a tremendous amount of guilt because I couldn't honor Ellen's last wishes. Several times I nearly caved in.

'All my life I've had to settle for second-best and I didn't want to force you to do the same. After J.D. offered his home to me I knew I wouldn't be content. J.D. is a wonderful man, and he'll be great for Daniel, but I want first place in someone's heart.'

Tristan rose, pulling her up with him and enfolding her in his embrace. He lowered his head to whisper in her ear, 'You've got it. First place and, until the children come, the only place. Is that good enough?'

Shielded from the wind, she buried her nose in his massive chest and nodded.

His voice became thoughtful. 'If you refused Berkley right away then why did he imply that you were considering his offer?'

'Maybe he thought one good turn deserved another.'

'Maybe so.' He lifted her chin to stare into her eyes. 'Will you marry me? Not for Daniel's sake, but our own?'

'Oh, yes.'

His mouth latched onto hers. She hardly noticed his cold skin against her cheek, reveling in the heat his lips created.

'Come on, you two,' the deep voice of a night security guard broke in. 'Take it home. This is a hospital, for heaven's sakes. Not lovers' lane.' Muttering about the shamelessness of adults who should know better, he disappeared through the automatic doors.

Tristan tucked Beth under his arm. 'The man said to go home. Shall we?'

She smiled up at him, her heart as light and bright as the twinkling stars overhead. 'Doctor knows best.'

'Are you ready, Beth?' Naomi asked, fussing with the train of Beth's wedding gown.

'You bet.'

'Tristan must have worked miracles to get the arrangements made so quickly,' Kirsten commented. 'Christmas is such a popular time to get married.'

Beth smiled. 'I think Tristan pulled a few strings. He was determined to have our wedding this month. I was too.'

The music started. Naomi and Kirsten filed in as her bridesmaids. Soon the organist played the familiar notes, the piece Beth had dreamed of hearing on her special day.

She took one step, then another, inching her way down the aisle toward the tall, handsome man waiting near the altar. She hardly noticed the room full of guests, the red poinsettias decorating the chapel and the candles winking in the background. Out of the corner of her eye she caught a glimpse of Daniel, perched on J.D.'s shoulder.

Tristan stepped forward. He took her hand and threaded her arm through his, before turning to face the hospital chaplain.

Beth's heart swelled with happiness. She couldn't think of anything she'd rather do than gift the man beside her with a promise to love and cherish. After all, she'd been waiting for him her entire life.

Look next month for Kirsten's story in
A HEART OF GOLD
as she meets up with Dr Jakob Marshall
in the second of the *Sisters at Heart* trilogy

*We hoped you have enjoyed this month's Medical Romances™ from our **'Rising Stars'**—four talented new authors.*

To ensure we continue to provide you with the very best in Medical Romances, please spare a few minutes to answer the following questions. Your comments are very much appreciated. Please tick the appropriate box to indicate your answers.

HINKING ABOUT THE MEDICAL ROMANCE STORYLINES, THERE:

Too much medical content ❑
Not enough ❑
Just right ❑

Are the medical references too technical? ❑
Not technical enough ❑
Just right ❑

Are the stories: Too sensual ❑
Not sensual enough ❑
Just right ❑

Do you like settings in the UK ❑
Foreign Countries ❑
Don't mind ❑

Do you like stories that are linked to other books?
e.g. Flying Doctors, Camberton Hospital Y ❑ N ❑

How long have you been a Medical Romance reader?
Less than 1 year ❑ 1-2 years ❑ 3-5 years ❑
6-10 years ❑ Over 10 years ❑

Do you read any other Mills & Boon® series?
Please tick the series you read

Presents™ ❑
Enchanted™ ❑
Historical Romance™ ❑
Temptation® ❑
By Request™ ❑
Others (please specify) ❑

8. How many Medical Romances™ do you read/buy in a month?

	Read	Buy
1-4	❑	❑
5-8	❑	❑
9-12	❑	❑
13-16	❑	❑

9. Thinking about the new white Medical Romance covers, do you:

Like it very much ❑ Don't like it very much ❑

Like it quite a lot ❑ Don't like it at all ❑

10. Please indicate your age group

16-24 ❑ 25-34 ❑ 35-44 ❑

45-54 ❑ 55-64 ❑ 65+ ❑

THANK YOU FOR YOUR HELP

Please send your completed questionnaire to:

Harlequin Mills & Boon
Medical Romance Questionnaire
Dept M
PO Box 183, Richmond
Surrey, TW9 1ST

Ms/Mrs/Miss/Mr ______________________________

Address: ______________________________

____

______________________________ Postcode ______________

You may be mailed with offers form other reputable companies as a result of this application.
If you would prefer not to receive such offers, please tick box. ❑

MILLS & BOON®

Medical Romance™

COMING NEXT MONTH

ICURABLY ISABELLE by Lilian Darcy

abelle returns to her roots in France, determined to heal a ong-standing family rift, but, made apprehensive by a iend, she keeps her identity secret from her second cousin, acques—a mistake, when they fell in love.

IEART OF GOLD by Jessica Matthews
isters at Heart

irsten is committed to her clinic helping the poor, but its uture is uncertain. She reluctantly accepts the help of Jake, naware he is responsible for the uncertainty.

IRST THINGS FIRST by Josie Metcalfe
t Augustine's

ick can't face the anniversary of his wife's death; Polly won't t him give in, but when did comforting turn into love?

VINGS OF LOVE by Meredith Webber
ying Doctors—final episode

ase Manager Leonie had survived one bad marriage—loving lex was a risk, one she might not take, particularly if it eant living in Italy!

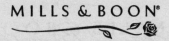

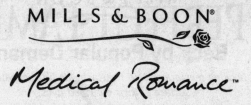